Loving My Miami Boss

Hassan & Nazariah's Love Story

D1521857

A Novel By
Miss Jenesequa

Text **ROYALTY** to 42828 to

join our mailing list!

To submit a manuscript for our review, email us at

submissions@royaltypublishinghouse.com

Text RPHCHRISTIAN to 22828 for our CHRISTIAN ROMANCE novels!

Text RPHROMANCE to 22828 for our INTERRACIAL ROMANCE novels!

For all those that continue to support and rock with me. I love you guys more than you could ever imagine honestly. Thank you for purchasing my works and just rocking with my freaky shit.

Thank You God, for guiding me and strengthening me always.

"Don't be scared about putting yourself out there. You can offer something unique that no one else can, and someone will need." - @BossBabe.inc

—

- Jouir de! -

Miss Jenesequa

BY MISS JENESEQUA

- *Lustful Desires: Secrets, Sex & Lies*
- *Sex Ain't Better Than Love*
- *Sex Ain't Better Than Love 2*
- *Luvin' Your Man: Tales Of A Side Chick*
- *Down For My Baller*
- *Down For My Baller 2*
- *Bad For My Thug*
- *Bad For My Thug 2*
- *Bad For My Thug 3*
- *Addicted To My Thug*
- *Addicted To My Thug 2*
- *Addicted To My Thug 3*
- *Love Me Some You*
- *The Thug & The Kingpin's Daughter*
- *The Thug & The Kingpin's Daughter 2*
- *Loving My Miami Boss: Hassan & Nazariah's Love Story*

Loving My Miami Boss

MISS JENESEQUA

$ PROLOGUE $

"Get your sexy ass back in this bed, Nazariah. Now."

"No."

"Come here."

Nazariah quickly shook her head no at his sudden command. She didn't want to do anything now, realizing that even though he wasn't wearing a ring on his left hand, there was supposed to be one.

"I ain't gon' tell your ass again, Nazariah," he stated boldly, staring at her from where he lay. "Just come here."

"No," she whispered unconfidently, tearing her teary eyes away from his handsome face and shirtless body. "I'm leaving."

"No the fuck you ain't. A nigga hungry as fuck for you right now, and ready for you to come sit on his face all night, but now you wanna start actin' so dumb."

Without wasting another second to spare listening to him, Nazariah turned away from him and went to the glass table that she had left her silver purse on. She needed to get the hell up out of here. She couldn't allow herself to stay here with him alone. She could no longer stay up in this suite and mess around with him all night long in his bed. Allowing him to stretch her out and guide her into different positions while he slid inside of her, had to stop. Allowing him to kiss and touch in private places that he had managed to gain access to, had to stop.

"Nazariah, baby, chill," he whispered gently in her left ear.

How the hell had he managed to get out of his bed so quickly and creep up behind her?

"Hassan, no. You're ma—"

"But I'm fuckin' with you right now," he said, cutting her off and pressing his large hand onto her arm. "You the one I want, Nazariah."

The way his naked body was pressing up so close and hard to hers had her heart racing. She couldn't think straight with him this close. And the way his seductive scent was filling her nostrils, she knew she was going to get drunk in love because of it.

"I don't want this, Hassan. You're married, and I really don't want any problems in my life messing with you. So please let me..."

Shit.

Nazariah could feel him pressing his hard on directly on the curve of her butt. What the hell was he trying to do to her? Other than make her suffer for trying to leave him tonight.

10

"You don't want this?" he queried curiously, grabbing a hold of her arm and pushing her back closer to him so she was forced to stand still in front of him and feel his erection poking her ass. "You don't want this dick?"

Of course she did. She wanted every last inch of it. But it wasn't hers to want.

"Hassan, please..."

"Nah, please what? You the one tryna leave a nigga right now. You the one worryin' about shit that don't matter right now. What matters is you and I, no one else," he explained, moving his free hand in the gap between Nazariah's arm and waist, so he could place his hand on top of her flat stomach. Then, he slowly began moving his hand downwards towards the front of her blue thong.

"I've been craving that bomb ass pussy all day and now you wanna try and take it away from me? You must be crazy, girl."

She had purposely worn lingerie in his favorite color tonight, just to make him extra happy and excited.

Hassan suddenly pressed his lips against the side of her neck, quickly beginning to seduce her. He knew how weak she got to his neck kisses.

"Hassan oh... shit," she quietly moaned, unknowingly tilting her head to the side so that her neck was more exposed, providing him with much better access to kiss on her skin.

While he kissed, his hands went deeper past her thong and straight to her moist pussy lips.

When Nazariah felt his thick fingers beginning to play with her clit, she knew there was absolutely no going back now. He had won her once more.

Loving My Miami Boss

$ CHAPTER ONE $

To say the Dominican Republic was pretty would be an understatement. An absolute understatement.

It was absolutely beautiful, beyond beautiful in fact, just breathtakingly stunning. And Nazariah wanted nothing more than to stay here for the rest of her life. Too bad she was leaving in two days.

From the beautiful sandy beaches, the gorgeous greenery and the delicious food that she had been served, everything about the Dominican Republic was amazing to her. She had fallen in love with the culture, the entire location and the people; and she really didn't want to leave.

Nazariah slowly lifted her shades from her eyes and turned to face her best friend relaxing on the sun bed next to her.

"Amina, I don't want to leave," Nazariah informed her girl sincerely. "I really want to stay here forever."

"You and me both, girl," Amina announced, still keeping her eyes shut. "But you know duty calls."

As much as Nazariah hated to admit it, Amina was absolutely right. There was no way that they could afford to miss work. Both being nurses meant that the two of them had to be dedicated to their professions. Not dedicated to living la vida loca halfway across the world.

"We definitely need to come back though."

"Most definitely," Nazariah agreed.

"And next time, spend much longer," Amina added.

Nazariah nodded before turning away from Amina, so she could reach into her beach bag and bring out some more lotion. She continued talking though. "And a penthouse suite next time too, that the both of us can stay up there together with enough room for the both of u—"

"Aghhhhhh! What the fuck?!"

Nazariah suddenly turned back around to face Amina, to see why she had suddenly blurted out her anger.

She took one look at her friend and her eyes widened with surprise and worry.

Amina's pretty face was now drenched in water and it wasn't just her face. It was her entire bathing suit too.

Amina West wasn't your average chick. Not only did she have a smart mouth on her, something Nazariah had picked up from her, she was one very beautiful woman. Standing at 5'7", she had long, wavy, black hair that she had packed up into a messy bun, smooth, milk chocolate skin, a long yet well sculpted nose, honey brown eyes and large full lips. She also had a slim thick body, with thick thighs, a flat stomach and small breasts. Her butt made up for that though.

"Amina, what the... What just happened?"

"Someone just sprayed cold water all over me," she fumed. "And that someone is going to die. Tonight."

"Ain't nobody gonna be dying tonight, shorty, but I apologize about wettin' you up," a deep voice came from behind them both.

Nazariah and Amina turned around to face the voice only to stare up in complete awe at the shirtless handsome man now in front of them.

To say he was ugly would be a big fat lie. One massive lie! This man was undoubtedly handsome. He had to be at least 6 feet... No, even taller in fact.

His body had been cut to perfection. He had big muscular arms, just the right size that Nazariah liked. A rock hard chest of abs showcased on his light black skin, dark brown eyes, and a low fade on his round, slim head.

"I was havin' a water fight with my bro and he got a bit close to your bed. So when I aimed for him, I hit you."

Nazariah looked down at the large purple water gun that he was holding tightly in his hand. There was only one question on her mind as she kept silent and watched him. But Amina beat her to it.

"Ain't you a bit old to be having a damn water fight?"

"Says who?" he asked with an arched brow.

"Says me," she shot back coldly. "If you weren't having a water fight then you wouldn't have wet me now, would you?"

"Look, shorty, I'm old enough to do whatever the fuck I want," he snapped. "And if that includes having a water fight and wetting you up, then so be it."

"So you did this shit on purpose?" Amina fired back angrily.

"Nah... Actually, you know what? So what if I did?"

Amina immediately jumped up from her sun bed with a large frown. "You wet me up on purpose?!"

He slowly stepped closer to her with a sexy smirk. "And so what if I did? Besides..." His words trailed off as he looked her up and down, admiring her red swimsuit that complemented her sexy shape well. "You look good wet. Makin' a nigga wonder what else would look good wet."

Nazariah couldn't help but gasp at his freaky response. He had only amped Amina up with more anger though.

"Nigga, fuck you!"

"Fuck me? I'd love to see you do tha—"

"Khyree, what the hell is wrong with your dumb ass?"

And there *he* was.

Nazariah took one glance at him and swore she was in love. She swore upon it.

He was beautiful.

Just as muscular and as ripped as his brother, she was assuming that the guy who had wet up Amina was his actual real brother. They looked pretty similar too, except those eyes and the fact that he had a sleeve of tattoos on both arms.

He was fucking sexy, and the more she looked at him the more she felt like she was going to lose her mind staring at him. So she had to look away. But even looking away didn't help because she ended up looking right back and staring into those mesmerizing green eyes. He was also light skinned just like his brother, stood tall at about 6'2", had white, straight pearly teeth. He looked pretty young too, but even with his baby face, he was still so damn fine.

He also had a fade, but unlike his brother, he had curly soft hair coming out his head, and over his perfectly shaped, pink lips, he had a neatly trimmed goatee. In both ears a gold stud was in place, shining brightly at Nazariah. And in between his blue beach shorts, she couldn't help but notice that large bulge coming out of it.

"Bro, I came here to apologize to her, like you told me to. But her rude ass won't shut up now," Khyree told his brother.

"Your apology was bullshit and you know it! Right, Nazariah?" Amina stated boldly, dragging Nazariah into the conversation, making Nazariah groan in her head with disdain at the fact that she was now part of the conversation. She preferred staying quiet.

"Man, shut the hell up. My apology was sincere, but since your ass don't wanna accept it. I take that shit ba—"

"Khyree!"

"Nah, fuck her! Hassan, I apologized already. I to—"

"Khyree," Hassan affirmed, "apologize."

"Hell fuckin' nah."

"Now, Khyree!" Hassan loudly instructed.

Hassan.

Even his name was beautiful. She wondered how it would sound once she said it. How it would sound while he kissed every part of her body and fuck—

"I apologize for wetting you up," Khyree announced with a sigh. "It won't happen again."

"Damn right it won't," Amina stated, as she rolled her arms up against her chest.

"Nah, actually, it will happen again. Only next time it won't be your body I'll be getting wet," Khyree sexually remarked.

"Ohmygaaawd, I don't believe this fool. Nazariah, we're leaving!"

Amina reached for her towel and quickly began folding it up.

"One job, Khy. All you had was one job. Look ladies..." Hassan stepped in front of his brother and pushed him further behind. Towering over Amina he began. "On behalf of my dumb ass brother, I apologize sincerely on getting you wet Miss...?"

"Amina."

"Amina. If there's anything at all that you want me to do for you both," he said, flashing his eyes down to Nazariah with a sexy smile, "please don't hesitate to let me kno—"

"Yeah, yeah, save it, pretty boy. Me and my girl ain't got time for this. Nazariah, let's go," she demanded, staring down at her.

"Whoa, what's with all this animosity? I just apologized again to you, girl," Hassan commented with a mean mug.

"Apology not accepted. End of story," Amina responded sternly. "And it's Amina to you, not *girl*."

"Look, relax, girl. I don't get why you can't accept a simple ap—"

"Because she can't. End of story," Nazariah intervened, cutting him off.

She couldn't just sit back and not defend her girl. Regardless of if Amina was in the right or wrong, that was her girl of 15 years and she was always going to be there for her.

"I see you finally found your voice, Miss Shyness," Hassan responded coolly, making Nazariah frown. She got up to stand in front of him and looked up at him confidently. She was about to show him exactly why she wasn't shy.

"Fuck you and your brother's apology," she retorted, before swiftly picking up her towel and throwing it into her beach bag. "Come on, Mina. I'm ready to go."

"Right behind you, babe," Amina responded smugly, walking ahead and ready to head back into their hotel.

Just as Nazariah began following behind, she felt a hand pull on her arm. She turned around and looked down at the hand, only to stare up into the face of the man determined to speak to her.

"Firstly, I don't appreciate the way you or your friend have been treatin' my bro and I since we cam—"

"And I really don't care," Nazariah drawled, trying to pull away from his strong grip. "Let me g—"

He interrupted her and only held onto her tighter. "And secondly, I don't appreciate your ass constantly cuttin' me off when I'm trying to speak to you. Try that rude shit again and you gon' regret it, Nazariah."

The way he said her name instantly made her quiet. She couldn't believe how alluring and satisfying it sounded rolling off his tongue and coming out of his mouth. But his threat quickly brought her back to her senses and made her realize how crazy he was.

"You girls enjoy the rest of your stay now," he concluded, simply letting go of her before turning around and walking off with Khyree. Khyree shot Amina a cheeky grin before continuing to walk away from them.

Nazariah already couldn't stand his fine, rude ass.

What a jerk.

MISS JENESEQUA

$ CHAPTER TWO $

"Shorty rude as fuck. She lucky I ain't knock her stupid, sexy ass out."

Nazariah had Hassan completely fascinated.

"Shut up, Khyree. You know fully well we Knight Brothers don't hit women. So don't even try startin' that foul shit now, nigga, or you'll have me to answer to."

She was definitely a goddess.

One really attractive goddess that Hassan knew he wanted in his bed every night from this day forward.

She was a stunning, milk chocolate goddess with skin that looked so smooth and soft, making Hassan fantasize about all the kissing and touching he could do to her. Her hair was in single braids, but she had wrapped them all up into a neat bun. She stood at 5'9", pretty tall, but he still towered over her short ass. She had long legs with thighs so thick and juicy that Hassan badly wanted to grab hold of and wrap around his torso. Her ass wasn't the largest but those breasts of hers were perfect. Large, round with big chocolate tip nipples.

Those innocent brown eyes of hers had lured Hassan in the minute he took one look at her. That cute button nose on her face made him happier than a mothafucka, and he just didn't get why. And those lips looked so soft and kissable too.

He hadn't expected her to be so bold. Not at all. She seemed to be shy and one of those chicks that kept quiet at the first sign of trouble and just minded their business. Hence the reason why he called her Miss Shyness. Turns out, she wasn't Miss Shyness at all. And now because of that smart, fast mouth of hers, Hassan couldn't get her out of his mind.

"Man, whatever. I'ma get ready for the yacht party. Meet you downstairs in a few?" Khyree queried, bringing his fist out to dap with Hassan's.

"Bet," Hassan replied, dapping his brother.

The two split up and went into their separate penthouse suites to get ready for tonight's party.

The Dominican Republic was the Knight Brothers' party territory.

Whenever they came here on vacation, the whole entire island would automatically know who they were and what they were capable of. And let's not forget, they knew how wealthy they were too. Because of all these things, the Knight Brothers were always treated with nothing but respect. So for Nazariah and Amina not to treat them with respect and know exactly who they were had them both surprised. But Hassan was not only surprised by Nazariah not knowing who he was, he was also turned the fuck on. She didn't know who he was and what he owned. She didn't know all about the large abundance of wealth he gained on a daily and what his role was in Miami. She wasn't aware of who he was. And he loved that shit.

Other chicks would have died at the fact that the Knight Brothers had actually looked their way and decided to holla at them. But Nazariah and her girl hadn't flinched a bit. Not one single bit.

He wasn't sure if he was going to talk to Nazariah if he saw her again. Who was he trying to kid? He knew for sure that he was going to talk to her. Possibly just mess around and frustrate her some more. He liked seeing her angry because she looked so cute when she was mad, and the way her cute nose would flare up.

He wasn't sure when he was going to see her again but because they were both on the same island, he knew that she was definitely going to pop up soon.

But for now, Hassan decided that the best thing for him to do would be to get his mind off Nazariah and get ready for the yacht party he was heading to tonight.

He was definitely excited for it.

Half an hour later, Hassan had changed into a navy short sleeved shirt, white shorts and matching white J's. He also opted for silver studs, a silver chain, and his silver diamond Rolex. Then, he headed right down to meet up with his brother for their sinful night of fun.

*****

"What time does it start again?" Nazariah queried, as she applied her last coat of mascara.

"It started since seven," Amina replied, fixing her dress in the mirror in front of her. "It's now 10:30. We gotta get going, girl."

"Yeah, give me a minute," Nazariah said as she closed her mascara tube.

"I really hope we don't run into those fools again."

"What fools?" Nazariah questioned like she didn't know. She knew exactly what fools Amina was on about.

"Hassan and what's his face?"

"Khyree?"

"Yeah, him," Amina answered with a frown. "Both as dumb and rude as each other."

28

"But hella fine, right?"

"Annoyingly fine," Amina groaned. "That's what angered me the most."

"That they were fine?"

"And cocky as hell. You can tell they're the type of guys to have lots of girls flocking to them. They're used to getting what they want too. And those Rolex watches… I could almost smell how rich they were," Amina commented. "As much as I hope we don't run into them again, I have a big feeling we're going to see them tonight."

"And if we do, we just ignore them," Nazariah suggested simply. "They may be super fine and super rich, but they're super jerks. And you know what our rule is girl, we don't…"

"Fuck with jerks," Amina concluded, finishing off the sentence for her. "I know, I know. But there's just something about Khyree… that I can't shake off. I was only rude to him because I was pissed about getting wet. But then he started saying those freaky comments, which slightly turned me on but only made me mad. He makes me so mad but at the same time, he makes me want him even more."

"And that's what he wants," Nazariah explained. "For a sexy, single lady like you to fall madly in love with him so he can have you in his bed by midnight."

"Ha! Easy for you to say Miss 'I'm taken but my nigga really ain't shit.' I saw the way Hassan was looking at you and the way you were looking at him too. He definitely likes yo-"

Nazariah cut her off. "I really don't care, Amina. Me and Ant literally just got back together after he fucked up, and I really want to make things work between us. He might have cheated but I'm not about to follow suit and do the same."

Anthony was Nazariah's boyfriend of two years and despite all they had been through, she still had faith in him and their relationship. He had done her dirty but still she decided to give him a second chance.

"Once a cheater, always a cheater," Amina sang. "But hey, it's up to you. All I'm saying is, that man definitely wants you and you know what they say… What happens on vacation, stays on vacation."

Nazariah rolled her eyes at Amina's reflection through her mirror. "I really can't believe you're encouraging this right now, Mina. You're something else."

"I don't see nothing wrong with a little bump and grindddddd," she suddenly sang, swaying her hips to her own music in her head. "With a little bump and grinddddd."

"Girl, let's go before you start turning even more crazy," Nazariah voiced amusingly as she got up out her seat.

Fifteen minutes later, the girls had finally arrived at the boat and were granted access into the yacht party.

The boat looked really suave and glamorous. It was a large white boat with candles lit everywhere, providing everyone with sight to see in the dark night, red shiny glitter seats for people to sit on, bartenders and servers dressed in silver clothes, and a dance floor the size of Nazariah and Amina's hotel rooms put together.

"Damn, look at all these people," Amina announced just before a server came up to them with a tray filled with champagne glasses. "Ooo, don't mind if I do," she said, smiling as she took a glass.

Nazariah grabbed herself a glass too, before eyeing the free red chairs close to the dance floor. "Amina, let's go grab a seat."

Amina willingly nodded as she sipped on her champagne before following right behind Nazariah.

Just when they had gotten to their seats and started to get comfortable, their favorite song began to play.

Work, work, work, work, work, work

He say me have to

Work, work, work, work, work, work!

He see me do me

Dirt, dirt, dirt, dirt, dirt, dirt!

"Uh-uh," Nazariah began, watching as Amina's eyes widened with happiness. "Girl, don't start."

"Yaasss! This is our song, girl, we gotta go!"

By "gotta go" Amina meant that she wanted to go the dancefloor right now. But Nazariah had just gotten comfortable in her seat and getting up was not an option right now.

"Amina, no."

"Yes!" she exclaimed, jumping up and pulling Nazariah out of her seat. Leaving her with no choice but to follow her best friend. "We have to!"

As soon they arrived on the dance floor, all eyes were on them. Not just because of how excited Amina was but because of how good the both of them looked. They had decided to both sport matching dresses, just in different colors. Nazariah wore red whereas Amina wore blue. It was a curve hugging, high-knee sleeveless dress, that had a low revealing neckline, showing just the right amount of cleavage for the both of them, especially Nazariah. Their legs were out on display too and they were wearing the same Yeezy Season 2 beige heels.

No time to have you lurking

Him ah go act like he don't like it

You know I dealt with you the nicest

Amina began to move her hips seductively to the music, grabbing onto Nazariah's hands and making her dance with her. Nazariah had no choice but to follow pursuit, winding and moving her hips in time to the beat. She couldn't help it. "Work" was her jam!

They both began singing to the music too, still moving sexily as they did so with all eyes on them, as they danced in the middle of the dance floor. Two decent looking Dominican men came up to them with large smiles and before they knew, they were grinding their butts happily away on them.

Nazariah was just glad that they hadn't run into Hassan and Khyree. She figured that they weren't at this yacht party, so she wouldn't have to worry about them tonight.

But she figured absolutely wrong.

MISS JENESEQUA

$ CHAPTER THREE $

"Yo, ain't that th—"

Hassan immediately interrupted his brother. "Oh, that's them alright."

Both Hassan and Khyree were at the top VIP level of the boat, watching from above, the main dance floor below. They had actually been having their own exclusive party of their own, with a few ladies in nothing but their bathing suits. But the sudden excitement they could hear from down below had them intrigued. So intrigued that they had to take a peek. Now they couldn't tear their eyes away.

Hassan couldn't take his eyes off Nazariah. Damn, she looked good! Nah, she looked more than good, she looked fine as fuck! What the hell was she trying to do to him wearing such a sexy, little, tight dress like that? With those legs all out on display looking juicy. Yeah, she was really trying to kill him tonight. Those beautiful tits of hers were out too. Yeah, she was about to make a nigga lose his mind tonight.

And the way she was dancing with her girl, that only got him and his big guy down there very excited. He wanted nothing more than her dancing on him.

But jealously instantly clouded his thoughts once he noticed her excitedly grinding her ass on some random dude. Why the hell was she letting some random feel up and touch up on what belonged to him? She just didn't know it yet, but every single part of her now belonged to him. He was claiming it all now. And tonight, he knew he had to put that claim to action.

"You wanna go down, Khy?" Hassan asked Khyree curiously, already knowing his answer. He had seen the way Khy had been looking at Nazariah's girl, Amina, from this afternoon at the beach. He knew he had wet her on purpose because Hassan hadn't been anywhere near her sun bed. He just wanted to use it as an opportunity to talk to her.

"Fuck yes," Khyree answered firmly. "Let's go."

Nazariah and Amina were way too busy, living it up and enjoying themselves with the two dudes holding onto their waists and letting them dance their asses on them. Way too busy to notice the Knight Brothers standing a few distances away and observing them closely.

But they definitely noticed the atmosphere change on the dancefloor once "Work" by Rihanna stopped playing and Drake's "One Dance" came on instead.

Grips on your waist

Front way, back way

You know that I don't play

The two men that they had been dancing with suddenly left, and just before Nazariah could grab hold of Amina's hand to head back to their seats together, Nazariah felt her body being spun only to land directly into the chest of somebody else.

"What the…" Her words instantly trailed silent once she looked up from the hard chest, straight into those dark green eyes that she hadn't been able to get off her mind. "You again."

"What's that supposed to mean?" he asked with a frown, wrapping his arms around her curvy hips. "Miss Shyness not happy to see me?"

"Quit calling me that," she retorted, unable to break her eyes off those mesmerizing eyes. Why was he so fine? Even finer than when she had seen him on the beach this afternoon. Shit, she wanted him.

"You don't like me callin' you Miss Shyness?"

"No," she snapped.

"That's too bad," he responded calmly before leaning down low to whisper in her ear. "Because tonight I plan to call you whatever the fuck I like, especially when I'm bending you over and fuckin' you in my bed, Nazariah."

She almost fainted on the spot after hearing those explicit words leave his mouth. She even liked hearing it come out his mouth. But as quickly as she liked it, she hated it. Who the hell did he think he was?

"What the hell? No, you won't be doing any of that tonight," Nazariah fumed.

He chuckled lightly as he lifted his head up away from her ear, staring down at her before stating, "Says who?"

"Says I."

"You sure 'bout that?" he asked with a sexy smirk.

"I'm 100% sure about it… What the…Hassan, let go of me," she demanded, but it was too late. He had already turned her around and wrapped his arms tighter around her. She could already feel his erection poking her behind. He began to rock her body in time with his.

"So you can dance with other niggas but you can't dance with me?"

"I don't dance with jerks," she responded, looking straight ahead to see Amina and Khyree. By the looks of things, they were arguing. *Again.* They were looking and moving like a married

38

couple already.

"You think I'm a jerk?"

"I know you're a jerk," she insisted boldly. "That bullshit you said on the beach this afternoon proved that to me."

"It wasn't bullshit though. I don't appreciate bein' cut off at all. It's not somet—"

"Well, get used to it," she said, cutting him off.

Hassan decided to keep silent and continue moving his body in tune with hers. She was way too bold and strangely enough, he was digging it. Her sweet, fruity scent filled his nostrils and he couldn't help but push closer into her body as they danced together. She smelt so good. He could smell her all night.

"See Miss Shyness, I already told your ass once 'bout cuttin' me off," he reminded her smoothly. "But to have to remind you twice? That means I'm gon' need to teach your ass a lesson."

"A lesson?" she laughed. "How exactly do you plan to do tha... uhh," a sudden quiet moan escaped her mouth at the touch of his hand on her butt and his thick lips landing on the side of her neck. Before she could make out what he was up to, she felt a sudden sharp bite on her soft skin. And the shit had her pussy gushing quicker than water from a tap.

"Damn, you sound so fuckin' sexy when you moan. I can't wait to hear more of that shit tonight."

Goddamn it… this man wasn't just fine as hell; crazy, but also a seducer.

Nazariah lightly gasped once she remembered where they were. Where she was. She instantly broke away from Hassan, now determined to get Amina and getting the hell out of here. She would no longer be able to think straight knowing that Hassan was at the same party as her.

"Amina, let's go," Nazariah told Amina as she came to stand next to her.

"No, I'm not ready to leave yet, girl. Besides, I'm not done explaining to this idiot how stupid he is for coming up to me tonight."

Nazariah looked from Amina to Khyree, only to see an annoyed expression on his handsome face.

"All I wanted to do was apologize once more to your dumb ass and have a dance. What's so hard about that?" Khyree questioned with rage.

"What's hard about it is that you're an annoying fool, who just doesn't know when to quit!"

"Oh please, you know you want me," Khyree boasted. "Admit it."

"No, I won't! I don't want you!"

Nazariah sighed with defeat before deciding to leave Amina and Khyree right to it. They were clearly loving annoying the shit out of each other, and she would rather just stay right out of it until they were done. Then she would head straight back to her hotel room with Amina, because there was no way she was going alone.

Nazariah decided to head back to her seat, glad that Hassan seemed to have disappeared. He was nowhere in sight. And as she sat down and drank her third glass of champagne, she scanned her surroundings still unable to see where he had gone off to.

She still wasn't over the fact that he had bit her. As much as it hurt, it hurt so good and quite frankly, she wanted him to do it again. She was quickly becoming sprung on this guy and she didn't like it one bit.

You have a boyfriend waiting for you back in Miami, Nazariah. She knew this, but even knowing this, it was not stopping her from having the dirtiest thoughts about Hassan and being in his bed tonight.

Why was he such a jerk? A fine, sexy and dominating jerk.

"You better slow down with all those drinks, Miss Shyness."

The sudden sound of his deep voice made her jump in her seat with surprise, only to quickly stare behind at him smiling cheekily at her.

"You just don't know when to quit, do you?" she mumbled.

"If I see somethin' I know that I want, then I ain't gon' stop 'til it's mine," he announced confidently.

"And what is it that you want?"

"I want you, Miss Shyness."

"Will you stop calling me that? My God," she groaned.

"Like I said before…" he started, walking from behind her and taking a seat next to her. "…Tonight I plan to call you whatever the fuck I like."

"While you're fucking me, right?"

He smirked at her before answering, "What?"

"You forgot that part. From what you said earlier."

"Nah, I ain't forget," he voiced simply. "I knew you remembered though."

"Well too bad for you, I'm a lesbian."

42

His eyes widened with surprise. "You are?"

She nodded, removing her eyes off his so he wouldn't stare too deeply into her and realize that she was lying.

"So you tellin' me you only like pussy?"

Damn, even the way he said pussy had her getting hot again. Hot with desire and lust for him. He just didn't understand what he was doing to her. His entire presence was driving her insane.

"Yeah," she quietly responded, about to take another sip from her champagne when her glass was immediately swiped out of her hand.

Before she could make sense of the situation, she felt herself being pulled out of her seat and being dragged across the boat, through the crowd of people, to a completely different place that she had no clue about.

"Hassan, where are you taking me?"

He ignored her and just continued to lead her to the one place that he had been itching to take her to since he had first laid eyes on her on the dancefloor.

Once rushing her up a short flight of white steps, Nazariah realized that he was taking her to a private closed off area to the rest of the public, guarded by a single security guard. And once arriving on the top deck to an empty floor level, her heart began to race with nervousness.

It was a stunning top deck with a gorgeous view of the blue sea. Candles were lit all around and in the center sat a red circle cabana bed with white curtains hanging around it and gold pillows neatly arranged on it. There was also a nearby white table, with an ice bucket of more champagne and two empty wine glasses.

"You tryna get me drunk, jerk?"

"That depends… Are you already drunk?"

Nazariah shook her head 'no' before looking down at her hand only to see that her and Hassan were still holding hands. The second she tried to unlock her hand out of his, Hassan pulled her closer towards him until she was directly in front of him.

"I think I'ma like you drunk," he whispered seductively to her.

"Oh, so you can take advantage of me?" she asked, looking up at him and quickly getting lost into those green eyes again. "Real smooth, jerk."

"Uh-uh, I don't need alcohol to take advantage of you, Nazariah," he explained.

"So what do you need, Hassan?"

He dipped his head closer down to hers before responding, "You with me alone, no one else around."

Nazariah couldn't help but smirk. "That's all you need?"

"And that pussy drippin' for me."

Shit.

Nazariah's heart only began to increase with more speed and nerves. What the hell was he trying to do to her? Give her a damn heart attack?

"I'm not... I-I'm no—"

"Your pussy ain't drippin' for me right now, Nazariah?" he queried curiously, pressing his body even closer to hers.

"No, it's not," she firmly answered.

"I don't believe you."

"It's n—"

Her words were instantly silenced once Hassan's soft lips pressed onto hers. And the second she felt them on hers, she was a goner. There was no way she could fight it, especially with how much of a good kisser she quickly realized he was.

The kiss was sweet at first. But a few seconds into it, it quickly turned into a heated battle of lust and passion. His lips led the battle, seductively moving over hers before using his tongue to probe his way past her lips and collide their hungry tongues together.

Just when Nazariah felt his hand leave hers and the kiss get even deeper, Hassan suddenly pulled his lips away from hers before grabbing hold of her chin and forcing her to stare up at him.

"See, I knew your ass ain't no lesbian," he taunted.

"And how did you work that out?" Nazariah shyly asked.

"Ain't no lesbian gon' kiss me that good."

She bit her lips sexily at his words.

"Also…" Nazariah deeply sighed once she felt his warm hand move up her thigh. "Ain't no lesbian gon' get this wet for me that quick," he added before reaching the middle of her panties and pressing into her wetness.

She continued to bite her lips, only turning Hassan on even more.

"Stop doing that shit, Nazariah," he ordered, seriously.

"W-what?" she answered nervously.

"Stop biting those sexy lips of yours like that, making a nigga wanna do all types of freaky shit to you."

Fuck it, Amina was right. This man wanted her and despite the fact that she had a man at home, waiting for her to get back from her vacation, she wanted this man standing in front of her too. There was no point of denying it any longer. She wanted Hassan.

"What type of freaky stuff?" she asked in a low, innocent whisper, knowing exactly what she was starting right now.

Hassan looked down at her with curiosity and excitement at her words. He wasn't expecting her to ask him that. Honestly, he wasn't even sure if she was willing to go any further with him, and he wasn't planning on forcing her to do shit that she didn't want to do.

But he knew now for sure that she definitely wanted him.

MISS JENESEQUA

$ CHAPTER FOUR $

Hassan took one last glance at her before bending down low in front of her and lifting his hands to her warm thighs. Finally, he was doing the one thing he had wanted to do when he first met her: touch on those juicy thighs.

Once reaching the edge of her dress, he slowly lifted it up until it was above her hips, and then he pulled down her red thong.

Nazariah didn't know what had come over her to be allowing a complete stranger to be taking her underwear off. But she knew she wasn't about to stop him now.

"Hassan," she called to him, looking down at him nervously.

"Do you trust me Nazariah?"

Did she trust him? She had just met him a few hours ago and already they were in his private area of the yacht, and he had already pulled her thong down to her ankles. She didn't know what it was about him, but he had her sprung already.

She simply nodded at him.

"Then trust me enough when I say tonight, I promise to make this night the best night of your life so far. I'ma make sure you feel good tonight and do everything to have that pussy rainin' for me."

Nazariah felt herself getting hotter and wetter after his announcement, and all she could do was smile and nod at him.

She guessed she belonged to him tonight. Only for tonight though. What was the harm in that?

Seeing that she was down with what he had said, Hassan leaned in closer to her exposed hair free pussy, before gently kissing the top of it.

Her shit didn't smell and it looked good too, only enticing him further to start their freaky night of fun.

Tonight she was all his.

He didn't waste a second to spare. He just dove right in, not giving Nazariah the opportunity to process anything.

"Ugh! Ha… Hassan!"

The second his tongue hit her wet clit, Nazariah felt like she was about to faint with joy. The feel of his tongue was electrifying, almost indescribable.

All she could do was grip onto the back of his soft, curly head and cry out in pleasure with what he was doing to her.

"Hassan, shit," she whimpered once she felt his tongue move faster on top of her pussy.

He had just started and already he had her legs shaking for him. Now that he was getting a taste of her, he was quickly becoming addicted. Her sweet juices running down his tongue only encourage him to suck and lick on her faster. All he wanted to hear was her moaning his name, and now that he was finally hearing it, he wanted to hear it over and over again.

"Fuck, that... that feels so good," Nazariah announced in a half moan, looking down at Hassan as he continued to devour her.

She only became more turned on seeing his whole mouth latched onto her pussy and those lustful green eyes staring right back at her. Their eyes remained locked and Hassan could feel his erection growing, as he watched Nazariah's looks of pleasure overcome her. He loved the fact that he was making her feel this good right now.

Talented wasn't the only word Nazariah could use to describe how good Hassan was at giving head. He was more like a skilled, talented magician that knew all the right tricks to get her creaming for him even more. Even though he had only met her tonight, he knew everything to drive her mind insane.

Once his tongue started thrusting in and out of her tight hole, Nazariah wanted to scream out in ecstasy at how good it felt. But instead of screaming, she bit her lip hard and gripped onto the back of his head tighter, pushing him even closer to her treasure. She didn't want him to stop giving her this intense, amazing feeling.

"Mmmh." The sudden sounds of Hassan moaning against her pussy as he ate her out, only had Nazariah's horny state flying through the roof. He was the only man who had ever had her feeling this high during oral.

Nazariah felt her heart racing further once his tongue rapidly pushed in and out of her pussy. And her juices only began to flow quicker out and straight into his mouth. She could also feel her climax coming real soon and as much as she wanted this pleasure to last forever, she knew it was coming to an end.

Quickly, roughly grabbing onto the back of his curls, Nazariah pulled Hassan's head back only so she could control the way she rode his face. She began writhing against his face, loudly moaning his name, as the intense pressure inside her began to build.

Hassan only found himself becoming more turned on seeing that Nazariah was now taking control of the situation. Usually, he dominated but tonight, she could get it popping however the fuck she wanted. Only for now though.

As she controlled the way she rode his face, he lifted his hand higher up her thigh before sliding round to the back of it and reaching the curve of her ass.

"Agh, fuck! Uhhh."

Hassan suddenly smiled at the way Nazariah's mouth had parted slightly and her eyes began to roll backwards, as he pushed his finger in her butt and quickly began pushing it in and out of her.

In all her sexual encounters in this lifetime so far, Nazariah had never had a finger up her butt. She would have never thought about having one in there and if she had, she would assume that it would hurt. But strangely enough, Hassan putting one in her now had her emotions flying through the roof and her juices constantly gushing out her pussy. It felt good!

"Hassan, I'm about to…" Her lids became heavy and her head fell back with ecstasy as she felt her climax rush through her and hit straight below. She continued to rapidly ride his tongue as her climax came flowing out. "Ohhhh, goddamn it… Agh!"

Every single last of her sweet nectar that came cascading out of her, Hassan made sure that he drank every last drop up.

Nazariah wasn't even given a chance to properly process the overwhelming orgasm that she had just experienced. She had just experienced the best orgasm of her entire life. He didn't even give her a full minute to process it all because before she could get one, Hassan stood up and pulled her straight towards the red cabana bed.

And that's when the freak in him truly came out.

Nazariah felt him pull her dress up higher until it was over her head and completely off her body. He instantly chucked it to the side before pushing Nazariah onto the bed, still in her heels, making her get on her knees. Then he pushed her head down facing the gold pillows.

Just as he pulled close the white curtains, she remembered something very important. "Hassan, protection," she managed to whisper out shyly.

"Turn around," he ordered and she turned her head to the side to look back at his shirtless muscular physique. Only for her eyes to widen with fear as he covered his dick with a condom.

"Oh my…" Nazariah's words trailed off quietly as she continued to stare straight ahead at his manhood, poking out and standing at full attention.

Hassan couldn't help but chuckle at her reaction to his size. It was usually like that when ladies saw how much he was packing. Most were shook; some ready to back down and forget them having sex all together, and some very excited and already in love.

"Face down, ass up," Hassan firmly instructed. "Ain't no

54

runnin' now, Nazariah. You're all mine tonight."

Nazariah slowly did as he wanted, sending a quick prayer to the Lord above that she wouldn't break tonight. With how large his dick was, she was seriously worried. But as worried as she was, she was also excited.

"Especially since a nigga already had a taste of that bomb, tight ass pussy."

Shit. Nazariah knew tonight was going to be one wild night.

Slap! Slap! Slap!

"Shit," Nazariah whimpered out in pain after Hassan's hard spanks on her butt. She wasn't used to being spanked at all. But she had a feeling he was the type to spank during sex, so she knew she was going to have to get used to it.

Hassan remained still, on his knees high above her, causing her get uneasy awaiting for his next move.

"Hassan, I'm re… Ooooo, fuck."

His thick rod slowly entered her, filling her up quick and tight. Nazariah could already feel herself losing control of her emotions. The second he started moving, she couldn't control herself.

"Hassan, fuck yes," she continued to moan, not wanting to be too loud especially since they were still on the boat filled with people partying downstairs. But the loud music playing would mask her moans.

Faster and faster he pounded into her, watching the sexy sight of his dick thrusting in and out of her tightness. It all felt fucking fantastic.

"Shit, you so fuckin' tight, girl," he groaned, loving the way her tight walls clung around his thick length.

"Yasss, faster. Give it to me deeper." They had just started and Nazariah already couldn't get enough of him. She loved how deep and speedily he was fucking her. This nigga had her mind blown from the very first stroke and now she was obsessed. "Fuck me, baby."

"Just like this?" he questioned, pushing into her harder and deeper as his hand latched onto her moving hips. "This how you want me to fuck you, girl?"

"Yesss," she whispered lustfully, throwing her ass back onto him and beginning to twerk as he continued to fuck her. Hassan hitting it from the back had her on cloud nine right now. This wasn't even a position that she usually found herself in during sex. But right now, she was willing to do whatever to please him.

"Fuuck," Hassan groaned, loving the sight of her ass moving up and down his dick right now. What the fuck was she doing to him? "You bad girl… I see you."

Nazariah continued to moan, feeling herself get wetter and wetter the more he stroked his hard rod in and out of her. This nigga had her mind gone.

Hassan watched with delight as Nazariah suddenly began to arch her back for him. Her legs shook as he moved in and out of her, continuously slamming their bodies closer together. He couldn't stop groaning because of how right she was doing him.

"Damn, I love this shit."

Hassan aggressively grabbed hold of her braids after hearing her say that, forcing her head all the way back closer to him so that he could whisper closer into her ear as he fucked her.

"You love it?"

"Yesss."

"You love this dick, Miss Shyness?"

"I do, baby," she responded with a sexy smile, her mouth parting wider and wider with each thrust he delivered inside her.

"Tell me how much you fuckin' love it," he firmly demanded.

"I love it so much."

He grinned happily at her response before adding, "You still hate me callin' you Miss Shyness?"

Nazariah shook her head 'no', feeling her body get hotter and hotter. Both their naked bodies were beginning to glisten with small beads of sweat. She felt his hand unfasten its tight grip on her braids and immediately move to her throat.

"That's good," he seductively voiced, choking her, as his dick still eased in and out of her. "Cause like I said before, tonight I plan to call you whatever the fuck I like. You my little freak bitch for the night, Nazariah."

Hassan suddenly mushed her face down into the pillows and watched, as she bit into one trying to conceal her moans.

Yeah, he wasn't letting her or that pussy leave him anytime soon.

Loving My Miami Boss

$ CHAPTER FIVE $

"Yeah, shit… Ride that dick, just like that."

Hassan was completely over the moon with the fact that he had this goddess in his penthouse suite right now. After fucking her in every way last night at the yacht party and pleasing her in ways he hardly did with any chick, he had whisked her back to his suite just so that he could wake up happy, seeing her pretty face right beside him.

Everything about her was perfect to him.

From that body, that gorgeous face and that pussy, she was just perfect.

And now that he had had her more than once, he knew there was no way he was planning to stop anytime soon.

"Fuuuck," Hassan loudly groaned, watching her large breasts fly up and down as she rode his dick like a solider. He found himself becoming even more turned on when she grabbed his hand, put one of his fingers into her mouth and sucked on it hard. Making him heat up with desire at how good her mouth would feel around his dick.

When she placed one hand around his throat, Hassan's mind began to spin with an incontrollable desire. And he could feel his climax only approaching quicker.

Thirty minutes later, their third round of the morning was done and Nazariah quickly pulled Hassan's red silk sheets off her body.

Just when she made movements to leave his bed, she felt a hand on her arm, pulling her back.

She shyly turned around to stare into his green eyes.

"Hassan, I gotta go."

He instantly frowned at her words, pulling her closer to him in the bed until she was back into the position that he wanted her in: lying right next to him.

"Says who?" he queried sternly.

"I leave with Amina tomorrow," she explained. "I need to start packing."

From what she had told him already, Hassan had been made aware of the fact that Nazariah had already been in the Dominican Republic for six days. She was leaving tomorrow. But Hassan didn't want her going anywhere yet.

"Yeah, you need to start packing so you can move all your shit in here."

Nazariah shot him a confused look. "What?"

"Stay a little while longer," he suggested gently. "With me."

As tempting as his offer sounded, Nazariah wasn't sure she would be able to do it. She certainly wasn't looking to spend more money to extend her flight a couple more days... Just for some dick... Some bomb ass dick.

She shook her head 'no'. "I can't. That's more money and more days missed at wo—"

"No one said anything about you payin'," Hassan said, cutting her off. "Just say you'll stay and I'll take care of everything."

Nazariah nervously bit her lip, thinking about his offer and wondering if she should accept it. Now that he was willing to pay, what was really stopping her from staying a couple extra days?

"And if I say no?" she quietly asked, avoiding his hard gaze by staring down at their naked bodies underneath the sheets. His body still looked so attractive to her.

"You won't say no," he confidently announced.

She scoffed before staring up at him. "Says who?"

"Says I," he replied proudly. "We both know you want to stay."

"Let me think about it."

"What the fuck is there to think about?"

"I have a job, Hassan, a life..." Her words trailed off once she remembered Anthony. Her boyfriend.

"All things that are going to be waitin' for you when you get back," he commented.

As much as he assumed that what he and Nazariah had was a one-night stand, he couldn't bring himself to convince his mind of that. This might have been a one-night thing, but he didn't want it ending anytime soon. He just needed a couple more days with her and then he would be good. He was sure that she would be out his mind soon enough.

"Just let me think about it, Hassan, please," she softly pleaded before pecking his lips.

He simply nodded with a sigh before lifting a hand to her flat stomach and moving it upwards onto her left breast.

When he started to squeeze, Nazariah grabbed his hand and stopped him.

"I still need to go, Hassan."

She smirked as he rolled his eyes in annoyance.

"I need to check on Amina. I haven't seen her since last night, remember?"

"I'm sure her ass is fine," Hassan responded. "Khyree was keepin' her company."

"I still need to check on her," she repeated, pushing his hand off her body and quickly rolling away from him. Before Hassan could try and grab onto her, she was out his bed and stretching.

As she stretched, Hassan admired her naked figure once more, pleased that every last part of her body had felt his lips last night. She was so damn beautiful.

"You comin' back to let me know if you staying with me, right?" he queried, watching her put back on her dress from last night.

"Ummm, if you're lucky," she taunted, zipping up her dress.

"Nah, you are comin' back, Nazariah," he bossed.

"We'll see," she lightly sang, slipping into her beige heels again. She couldn't even keep still; her legs were tired out from all the sex she had been having. They felt like they wanted to just collapse.

"Don't make me come find your ass, Nazariah."

"Ooo... Is that a threat, Mr. Knight?" she questioned, observing him amusingly as he sat up in his bed closely watching her.

Despite all the sex they had been having it, Nazariah had managed to find out small details about Hassan. One of them included finding out that his full name was Hassan Knight.

"You damn right it is," he playfully snapped. "You make me come find you, you get punished."

Nazariah's pussy starting getting hot again. She was seriously considering making him come find her so that she could get punished.

His crazy, freaky self was just making her more addicted to him. One of the main reasons why she was apprehensive about staying alone with him some more. Could she handle him?

***

"You little freak," Amina exclaimed with joy, closing her book that she had been reading. As much as she loved reading, it could wait. Nazariah had just experienced a juicy night that Amina couldn't wait to hear all about. "Just look at you trying to walk straight and failing." Her laughter immediately filled the hotel room. "My best friend's pussy was finally murdered last night."

"Amina!" Nazariah gasped with her mouth wide before laughing too. "I really can't feel my damn legs." Nazariah quickly plopped herself onto the nearest sofa.

"That's how I know he was amazing to you last night," Amina said. "So, I need details! Tell me everything. From dick size, stroke game, the whole nine yards."

"Amina, later," Nazariah yawned. "I'm still so tired."

"And I really don't care!" she shouted. "You left me with that annoying fool last night."

"Khyree may be annoying but you love his ass now."

Amina slowly began to crack a smile. "He's still annoying."

"Did you have sex with him?"

"No... But after all the arguing, we shared a few drinks together, danced and talked."

"About?" Nazariah queried curiously.

"Just life and stuff. I was getting a bit tipsy though so I can't really remember half the shit I said. I'm praying I didn't say no dumb stuff though," Amina replied.

"I'm sure you didn't."

"But hey, back to you! Tell me everything," Amina demanded with excited eyes.

66

So Nazariah told her everything. From how Hassan dragged her to his private spot on the boat, smoothly seduced her and had her cumming for him within seconds. She told her about all the positions, all the words shared and how he wanted her to stay a little longer in the Dominican Republic with him.

"Okay, then say yes and tell him. He's already offered to pay so you don't need to worry about that," Amina reminded her coolly.

"What about my job? I still need to do that, remember? And Anthony, what wi—"

Amina cut her off. "Firstly, I will cover for you at work, earning you an extra week off. As for Anthony, that nigga already cheated on you, girl! He ain't shit, so stop thinking about him. You ain't never gonna see this fine nigga again, make the most of him now before he leaves your life for good."

Nazariah kept silent for a minute, contemplating to herself for a while. Amina was right about her not seeing Hassan ever again. She wasn't even sure what part of the U.S. he had come from, but she figured it wasn't Miami. He was probably from Los Angeles or New York, not Miami. She wouldn't ever see him again after this trip. So what was the harm in spending some more time with him?

Anthony hadn't thought about her when he cheated, Nazariah

could only do the same.

"I'm not sure I can handle him, Amina. I've been with him for a couple hours already and most of that has been on a bed. He's so dominating and... and quite frankly, I'm a little scared," she admitted truthfully.

"Scared? Scared of what?" Amina threw her a confused look. "It's about time you experienced a man like him, even if it is just for a little while."

"I guess I'm just used to being the dominating one," Nazariah explained.

"You sure are. Cause Anthony ain't nothing but a little bitch ass ni—"

"But he can be dominating at times," Nazariah intervened.

"Yeah, but not all the time," Amina fired back. "Hassan is dominating this whole entire situation and you don't know how to act. You've never really had a man tell you what to do, or control you in the bedroom; this is all new to you."

"Very new," Nazariah mumbled.

"But you're going to love it. Trust me. It'll only turn you on like it turned you on in his bed."

"It did, I won't lie."

"Well then, what are you really waiting for? Just give this a chance. It's only one extra week. Before you know it, you'll be back to your life with boring Anthony."

Nazariah sighed deeply at Amina's words. She wasn't sure exactly what she was going to decide, but her heart was telling her to stay with Hassan for just a couple more days...

***

"Damn, bro, you smashed already?"

Hassan simply nodded as he poured himself some coffee from the glass kettle.

"How was it?" Khyree asked with way too much curiosity and fascination in his voice for Hassan's liking.

"You know I don't like talkin' to you about that," Hassan voiced with a frown as he poured milk into his cup. "It's private."

"Man, fuck all that! I tell you about mine all the time."

"But do I ever ask you, Khy?"

"You still listen though," Khyree responded smartly. "Which is why I'm prepared to listen to you right now. How was she?"

Hassan simply kept quiet before taking a sip of his coffee. He wasn't one to brag about the chicks he messed with. Especially with his brother. That's just the way he was. He liked keeping those type of things private and to himself.

"Yo, with the way you acting, I bet it was wack. You would have said something already."

Hassan took one last sip from his coffee before placing his cup down on the marble counter behind him, and staring right at his brother through hooded eyes.

"You think it was wack?" he queried with an arched brow raised.

"I know it was wack," Khyree answered with a cheeky grin. "Cause if it wasn't, I wo—"

"For your information, it wasn't wack," Hassan snapped, instantly cutting his brother off.

"I don't be—"

Hassan cut across his words once more. "That pussy was the bombest shit I had had in a long time. A real long time. If I could marry the shit I really would. It had me on cloud mothafuckin' nine for the whole entire night, and I couldn't stop having it. Almost to the point that I don't want to stop having it. Shit, I even want it right now. Does that sound like some wack shit to you?"

Khyree quickly shook his head 'no' at his brother before shooting him a toothy smile.

"You ain't even know the chick that long and you're already sprung, San. You gotta be careful, bro."

"Sprung? Nah, I ain't sprung."

"Yes you are. You're sprung, one-hundred percent," Khyree insisted. "You said it yourself you even want her right now, right?"

"Yeah, but that's only because I want her again like I had her all last night," Hassan explained.

"And before you know it, you'll be wanting her in much other ways. Just not for the sex."

"No I won't," he disagreed.

But Khyree continued to shoot him a knowing look before shaking his head 'yes'.

"Yes you will."

"Oh yeah? So what about you and Amina? You looked like you were pretty sprung last night," Hassan commented smugly.

"Nah... She's cool and all, but I don't see it going any further than last night," Khyree responded.

"What happened last night?" Hassan asked as he shot his brother a curious look. Had he smashed Amina?

"Nothing other than us arguing, drinking and dancing a bit."

"So you ain't smash?"

Khyree shook his head 'no' before looking down at his hands, avoiding Hassan's hard gaze.

"Aha! And that's why your ass is so salty today," Hassan announced amusingly. "You mad you ain't smash her yet."

"No I ain't," Khyree protested. "I ain't!"

"Yes," Hassan insisted with a head nod. "That's why you so mad right now Khyree."

"I'm not mad!" he yelled. "Who even told you I wanted to smash her?"

"So you tellin' me right now, you don't want to smash her?"

"No," Khyree quietly answered.

"So why'd you wet her up yesterday? You and I know damn well I wasn't anywhere near her sun bed. You did that shit on purpose, Khy."

72

"Yeah, but that ain't mean I wanted to fuck her…"

Hassan simply chuckled and rolled his eyes at Khyree. He knew that his brother was lying. He had always been such a bad liar and now only proved that theory further. Khyree definitely wanted Amina and the fact that he hadn't had her last night in the way he usually had his chicks so fast, was why he was salty and down today, and being extra annoying, prying into Hassan's shit.

"Okay, look. I ain't gonna lie, I did want to fuck her last night," Khyree announced.

I fuckin' knew it, Hassan mused.

"But she didn't really seem into me, especially since when I first came to talk to her we immediately started going at it. And when all started going well, she got hella tipsy, constantly taking chugs of her champagne while we talked. I don't think she's feeling a nigga…"

"She was probably nervous," Hassan suggested. "Females tend to do that drinkin' shit a lot. Besides, if she wasn't feeling your dumb ass, I'm sure she wouldn't have continued to tolerate you the whole night. See all that arguing shit you be doing? Other females would have just said a few words and kept it moving, but she keeps throwing shit back at you, right? That means she likes you enough to keep coming at you the same way you're comin' at her. I'm sure she's feeling you, you just don't see it yet because you haven't had sex with her. Maybe sex isn't what you need with her."

"But you and Nazariah smashed so qu—"

"Who do you like, nigga? Amina or Nazariah?" Hassan questioned sternly, cutting him off.

"Amin—"

"Okay then," he retorted, sucking his teeth. "Worry about Amina then. I might have smashed Nazariah so quickly but that's only because she was down for it from the jump. We both wanted it. Amina just ain't ready yet, and if you like her as much as I think you do, then you'll wait 'til she is."

"A'ight, I hear you, bro," Khyree stated contently. "I still wanna spend some time with her before she leaves though."

"I told Nazariah to stay an extra week, maybe you should do the same," Hassan offered. "Tell her you want to get to know her some more or some shit like that."

"Did Nazariah agree to stay though?"

"Not yet, but she will."

"How you know?" Khyree queried with a tone full of wonder.

"Because I'm about to head to her hotel room and get her to

start movin' her shit into my penthouse."

"Right now, nigga? Damn, you already find out her hotel room and everything?"

"We own 65% of the hotel resort, nigga. Did you suddenly have amnesia and forget?"

Khyree smirked before asking, "Did you find ou—"

"Amina's room?" Hassan finished off for him with a sneaky grin. "It's the one next to Nazariah's."

Khyree's brown eyes widened with happiness.

"Put on a shirt and let's bounce," Hassan instructed.

He couldn't wait to see Nazariah already and make her get all her stuff together for moving into his penthouse. She was staying with him and that was the end of the discussion.

MISS JENESEQUA

$ CHAPTER SIX $

After having a long needed shower and grabbing some more rest for her aching body, Nazariah was fully awake and ordering some room service for her and Amina. Despite them having separate hotel rooms right next to each other, they did have sleepovers in each other's rooms during the past week. And since this was technically the last day of their vacation together, they were choosing to spend it together, in Nazariah's hotel room.

"What movie should we wa—"

Knock! Knock! Knock!

Three loud knocks sounded on Nazariah's hotel door, instantly making her and Amina think that room service had finally arrived.

"That'll be room service finally with our stuff," Amina happily stated.

"Yup." Nazariah got up from her seat and casually sauntered to the door. The second she opened up before even spotting his handsome face, she could feel him. She could feel his presence suddenly all around her, up in her personal space, and before she could fully process what was going on, her door was pushed wide open.

Shit.

Nazariah took one look up at his attractive eyes and wanted to collapse and faint. The same way she wanted to collapse and faint the first time she had laid her eyes on his fine self.

How the hell had he found out what room she was staying in?

"How the... What the..."

He sexily smiled before speaking up. "I told you not to make me come find your ass, Nazariah."

Damn, even with no makeup on and casual clothing, she still looked fine as fuck to Hassan. He was suddenly filled with the urge of whisking her back to his suite this instant.

Nazariah suddenly remembered his threatening but alluring words from before. He had said that if she made him come find her, he would punish her. And just by the way he was staring at her, biting his juicy lips at her too, she knew he was dead serious.

"I... I fell asleep," she sheepishly informed him, admiring the way his muscles and tattoo sleeves looked. Since he was sporting a fresh, white wife beater with grey sweats, she was getting a great view of his muscular physique.

"Well, I'm still gon' pun—"

"Yo! San, she's not in her room," a familiar voice from nearby Nazariah's room suddenly sounded. She immediately recognized

78

the voice as Khyree's and all she could do was smile once realizing that he had been looking for Amina.

"She's in here, fool," Hassan told him, turning to face his brother momentarily and nodding his head towards Nazariah's room. Then he turned back to look straight at Nazariah.

"You packed up your shit yet?"

"What shit?"

"Don't play dumb with me, Nazariah," he lightly snapped. "You know what I'm talkin' about."

"I still haven't made a decision."

"Yes you have," Hassan coolly voiced.

"Nah, Hassan, I haven't," Nazariah confidently responded. "Amina, Khyree's here to see you." She walked off away from Hassan, not bothering to see his facial expression as she went back to her seat next to Amina.

Amina shot her a surprised look and Nazariah simply ignored her, and focused on her bright plasma screen hanging on the nude wall in front of them.

Honestly, Nazariah wasn't sure how to feel or what to do at this moment in time. Now that Hassan and his brother had rocked up into her room, she felt angry, nervous and awkward all at the same time.

Angry because Hassan had found out her hotel room so quickly, nervous because of the fact that he was now here, in her space, watching her. And awkward because this was the man that she had been riding all last night—this morning too—and doing all types of freaky positions with. Now he was demanding that she move all her stuff into his suite, when she hadn't even had the opportunity to fully process what had happened between them both last night.

She didn't like it when things didn't go her way. Being an only child meant that Nazariah was used to things going the way she wanted. But with Hassan now, he was the one that was in charge of everything. He was dominating this whole situation and she just didn't know what to make of it yet.

Hassan didn't like the fact that he could sense Nazariah's cold attitude towards him. She seemed quite down this morning and open into spending some extra time with him, and he agreed to give her some time to think about it. But now it seemed like she wasn't wanting to spend some time with him at all. Her saying that she hadn't come to a decision yet was just some bullshit. She knew it, and he definitely knew it, too. She was just starting to play a game that Hassan wasn't willing to be a part of.

"Khyree, what are you doing here?" Amina questioned him, watching as he stepped deeper into the room behind Hassan.

"I just wanted to come kick it with you," he replied truthfully, moving to where Amina and Nazariah were seated. "And my bro wanted to come kick it with you, Nazariah."

While Khyree greeted Amina and started conversing with her, Nazariah kept her eyes far away from Hassan's and focused her attention on the bright screen ahead. She didn't give a flying fuck about Khyree and his stupid brother wanting to kick it with her and Amina.

Quite frankly, them both rocking up here had actually pissed her off. As much as she wanted to kick them out, she knew there was no point. They wouldn't want to leave and if they didn't want to leave, then they weren't going anywhere.

"You want something to drink, Khyree?" Nazariah offered Khyree, purposely not asking Hassan.

"Umm... Yeah, that'll be cool," he answered calmly.

"I want something to drink," Hassan suddenly spoke up.

"I don't recall anyone asking you if you wanted something to drink," Nazariah fired back with a pout. "Does anyone else recall?"

"What the hell is your damn problem all of a sudden?" Hassan

81

queried rudely.

"What's that supposed to mean?"

Both Amina and Khyree kept silent and just listened to the heated exchange now building between Hassan and Nazariah. They were both confused. Weren't these the two people having sex with each other all night long yesterday?

"Exactly what the fuck I just said," he fumed. "Why the hell you actin' so mean, Nazariah? Because I told you to move your stuff in my penthouse?"

"Because you got hold of my private room information without my permission."

"You knew what was gonna happen if I came lookin' for you," he explained. "My brother and I own a percentage of the hotel, we have access to everyone's room information. Not just yours. You ain't *that* special."

"Oh, so I ain't *that* special, huh?"

"Yeah," he quietly stated, knowing damn well that he was lying. He had only said that shit to fuck with her and it had definitely worked. She was livid.

"I ain't that special but you want me to spend a couple more days with you? Yeah, consider that definitely not happening now,

82

jerk."

Hassan sucked his teeth in annoyance. "So you don't want to stay?"

"No, why the hell would I want to spend some more time with you?"

"But you were willing to spend so much time ridin' this dick like a damn cowgirl, frontwards and backwards all last night," he commented with a frown. "You suddenly bump your stupid ass head and forget how much I made you cum last night? How much I had you screaming my name last night?"

"My stupid ass head?" Nazariah scoffed. Hassan had just amped her with much more anger and frustrations. And quite frankly, she no longer cared about Khyree and Amina listening in on this conversation. She was still going off regardless. "Nigga, you must have lost your damn motherfucking mind. Did you suddenly lose some common sense and forget how quick I had that dick cumming last night? You forget how much you kept reminding me how bomb my pussy was? You forget how many times you kept begging me to let you eat my pussy one more time?"

Hassan's jaw began to twitch and his fists suddenly clenched by his sides. As much as she was turning him on with this overly

MISS JENESEQUA

confident behavior of hers, she was also irritating him. He didn't want Khyree hearing this shit so he could use it later to tease him. But fuck it, she was the one that had started it.

"It's funny how you have so much to say now unlike yesterday when you had your mouth full with my dick in it."

Nazariah could feel her body getting hotter and hotter. She didn't like how easily he could get under her skin.

"Fuck you, Hassan," she barked.

"Fuck me? Yeah, you already did that shit," he commented with a fake yawn.

She officially hated him.

"I don't know why the hell you're yawning when you know fully well you enjoyed every last bit of us fucking last night," she announced proudly.

"Maybe I did, so what?"

"I hope you enjoyed every last second of it because that was the last time you'll ever get to touch me, Hassan."

Hassan's grin instantly began to fade after her words. Was she joking?

"What?"

4

"You heard me," she smugly replied.

Hassan couldn't believe it. What had started off as a heated yet amusing exchange, had now turned into Nazariah rejecting Hassan completely.

He decided on no longer saying any words to her and getting the hell up out of here. He was done with the bullshit and games.

"Khy, I'll catch you later," he informed his brother. "Amina, it was nice kicking it with you a bit."

"Ay bro, you're leaving?" Khyree questioned, watching as his brother got up from his seat.

Hassan nodded stiffly before heading straight for the door. He had had enough of this bullshit. Nazariah was over here playing games that he wanted no part of. She didn't want him, cool. He didn't want her either.

Seeing him walk towards her door definitely had her feeling some type of way. She hadn't expected him to get up and leave their building argument. She expected him to stay and continue to challenge her. But now here he was, doing the very opposite thing she wanted him to do.

Once her room door slammed behind him, Nazariah turned to face Amina and Khyree, who were both shooting her looks of disapproval.

"What?" she asked them both.

"You know you like him, Nazariah," Amina began. "Just stop fighting it and do what you want to do. Stay a bit longer with him."

"And I know for a fact Hassan likes you too. He doesn't usually act like this over just some ordinary chick. And you are definitely not just some ordinary chick. You even got the nigga smiling and shit. Hassan never smiles."

Maybe they were both right.

Nazariah just couldn't help but feel stubborn right now. It was in her nature to. But the chemistry and tension between her and Hassan wasn't unnoticed. The more he challenged her, that only riled her up with more emotion to challenge him. They were both two very dominant people and both extremely attracted to each other.

He had only gone through so much effort to find out her room number because he liked her. Nazariah knew it for sure.

Despite her claiming she hated him, she knew it could never be true. She didn't hate him. She only wanted him even more. She couldn't fight him off anymore.

***

Hassan was still pissed.

Leaving her hotel room and deciding to take a walk around the hotel before taking the elevator back up to his penthouse, didn't help clear his head at all. Because all he could think about was her. And how much mouth she had given him and how much he had hated it, but also loved it all at the same damn time.

No woman ever challenged or stood up to him like that. And no woman ever told him that she was no longer fucking around with him.

She's crazy, rude, but fine as fuck. You really think you can handle that right now? With all the shit you got going on?

Hassan wasn't really sure. And the more he relaxed on his deluxe beige sofa and took quick sips from his Corona, the more he couldn't get her out of his head.

Honestly, Hassan knew that the best thing for him to do would be to forget all about her. She said she wasn't going to stay with him and she was no longer messing with him, so it's best he forgot all about her. There was no point in thin—

Knock! Knock!

Hassan shut his eyes, trying to calm his frustration at the sound of two loud knocks on his door. It was definitely Khyree, following him back from Nazariah's, and probably down to tease him with all the things that Nazariah had blurted out.

So he decided to ignore it, hoping that Khyree would soon get the message and go away.

Knock! Knock!

But he didn't, only adding further to Hassan's rising frustrations.

The only way he was going to make Khy go away was by telling him to do so.

Hassan got out of his California bed, walked out his bedroom, past his living room, and straight to his front door.

Knock! Kno—

Just before the second knock sounded, Hassan's door flew open and before he could curse Khyree out, he looked ahead only to see an unexpected surprise.

It wasn't Khyree.

$ CHAPTER SEVEN $

Nazariah shyly looked up at him towering over her and couldn't help but feel herself swoon over him. She was never going to be able to get over how handsome he was. Never.

"What do you want?"

His question caught her completely off guard. Mostly because it was so rude, direct and blunt. And despite the fact that she had pissed him off, he was still down to talk to her.

After thinking to herself for a few minutes, Nazariah knew the right thing for her to do would be to go and see him.

"I came to apologize."

"Apologize then," he retorted.

She stared at him like he had lost his damn mind before calmly responding.

"And I apologize."

"For?"

"For hurting your feelings," she explained further, smiling slightly as she did so.

When she said it like that, she made him sound like a little school boy, unable to keep his emotions in check. She was just starting to be smart again and Hassan knew the only way to handle that smart ass, was to do what he said he was going to do in the first place.

Punish her.

"Is that all you came to say?" he curiously asked.

"Yes," she began before taking a deep breath and adding, "No..."

She couldn't believe she was actually about to do this. Even though she was scared as hell and still not happy about him randomly arriving at her hotel room, she still knew she wanted him.

"I want to stay," she whispered sheepishly.

Hassan's green eyes widened with joy. "You want to what?"

"I want to stay with you," she repeated. "I can only stay for five days though because of my jo—"

Nazariah's words were instantly shut up by Hassan's lips that were now locked onto hers. She had definitely missed the feeling of his soft lips of hers. As their tongues passionately meshed together, Nazariah felt Hassan pull her into his penthouse, shut his door behind her and push her onto his door.

"Five days is fine," he whispered sweetly as he pulled their lips apart. "Just let me hear you tell me one more time that you're staying."

"Why? You heard me already," she answered bossily.

Hassan only glared down at her before slowly moving his hand up her curvy waist. The sexual tension that had suddenly brewed between them both was uncontrollable.

Nazariah simply bit her lips before deciding to tell him what he wanted to hear. One thing she knew for sure about him, he loved getting his own way.

"I'm staying with you, Hassan."

A sexy smile beamed on his handsome face before he leaned in closer to look at her, making sure that this is what she wanted, and then locking their lips back together.

Five days and she was all his.

~ Three Days Later ~

He said damn bae you so little but you be really taking that pipe

I said yes daddy I do

Give me brain like NYU...

As Nicki Minaj's "Feeling Myself" played in the background behind them, Hassan gently nodded his head to the upbeat music before smirking down at Nazariah.

"Dance for me, baby."

"I already did."

"When?" Hassan's brow rose up in the air.

"You know when," Nazariah responded, reminding him of when she had danced for him in the bedroom last night. "How about you dance for me?"

Hassan shot her a crazy look like she had lost her damn mind or something, before softening his face a little.

"Yeah, I might, later, if you're lucky."

"Oh, I will be," Nazariah replied joyfully, licking her lips before moving in closer to Hassan's body.

Right now, they were having a private moment together on the beach, sunbathing on the same bed.

Hassan couldn't keep his eyes and hands off her. His arm tightened around her waist as he began to examine her. Seeing her wear such a thin, appealing black bathing suit had him feeling anxious. Anxious for her body, kisses, and, of course, that treasure in between her legs. He really couldn't wait.

And the fact that she had agreed to stay with him for the week still had him gassed. They had two days left with each other and the three days that had passed had been filled with nothing but mind blowing sex and them just having an overall good time together.

Hassan didn't want his time to end with her. He thought by getting her to stay a little bit longer with him would diminish the desire he constantly had for her, but it only made it worse. Much worse.

He really didn't want to leave her. In his dreams, he saw them both staying in the Dominican Republic for the rest of their lives. Not having to worry about going back home to whatever they had waiting for them. He was even considering doing it, but he knew he couldn't. Not just because of all the responsibility he had back in Miami but because Nazariah would never agree to it.

"Can we eat on the beach again tonight?" Nazariah queried.

Yesterday, Hassan had treated her to a midnight picnic on the beach and to say that she didn't like it would be a big fat lie. He was bringing out a side of him he rarely brought out because of her. His romantic side.

Loving My Miami Boss

"Your ass loved that shit too much," Hassan stated with a chuckle.

"Yeah, I did, especially desert," she whispered seductively to him before moving closer to softly peck his lips.

Nazariah couldn't get over the fact that in two days, she was never going to see this man ever again. And the fact that the two days were approaching so quickly was starting to make her real nervous. How was she supposed to say goodbye?

Amina had been dead right. Nazariah had fallen for her one-night stand. And if she was here now, she would probably convince Nazariah to spend some more time alone with him.

Amina had left three days ago to head back to Miami. She, too, had been considering to stay an extra week, but she didn't see the point. She had already enjoyed the Dominican Republic enough. What was she staying for? Especially since apparently Khyree never asked her to. So she headed back home and told Nazariah she would be seeing her soon.

"We can skip right now to desert, if you like," Hassan announced.

"Right now?" she asked feeling herself heat up with desire again for him. "What time is it?"

Hassan lifted his right wrist up to stare down at his gold diamond Rolex.

"It's 5:00 p.m.," he told her.

"In a bit, baby. Let's just chill for a while."

"Alright," he said, watching her gently close her eyes and remain as close to him as she could on the bed.

"Aren't you sick of me yet?" she randomly queried, her pretty eyes fluttering open to stare up at him.

"Do I look sick of you?"

"I don't know, that's why I'm asking," she explained simply, moving her fingers across his shirtless physique.

"Yeah, I'm sick of you," he blurted out before quickly adding, "Sick of how I can't get enough of you and how good you make me feel."

Nazariah smiled shyly before replying, "I'm sick of how you make me feel too. I feel like I've known you for years."

"Same," he agreed. "Just never met you yet."

"Where do you live?"

"Miami. I thought you already knew."

Nazariah's eyes widened with complete shock. "Wait, what?"

"I live in Miami," he repeated.

"So do I."

"Wait, what?" He too was shocked and the more he stared down at her in his arms, the more he realized that they hadn't told each other where they resided. "You do?"

She nodded enthusiastically. "I live there. Where about do you live?"

"Upper east side, Belle Meade."

"Damn... That's like the really rich area with all those gigantic mansions and shit," she commented, impressed with where he was living. From the second she first laid eyes on him, she knew he was quite wealthy; this only proved it to her further.

"Yeah, I guess," he answered with a light chuckle. "Where do you live?"

"Downtown Miami," she responded.

"In like a condo, right?"

"Yeah."

"Cool, cool."

"So what do you do? How'd you become so wealthy?" she curiously began to question him.

"I own a couple businesses here and there, one of them including this hotel," he coolly voiced, not wanting to give too much information away to her. It's not like he didn't trust her enough to tell her the true extent of what he did, he just didn't know how to tell her. And quite frankly, he was scared on how she would react. "A few investments too."

"That's good," she stated, still very impressed. This guy definitely wasn't just the regular guy she messed with. He wasn't no Anthony.

"And you're a nurse, right?"

"That's right. I see you remembered."

"Of course I did," he said, grinning. "There's only one person nursing this dick right every night."

Nazariah couldn't help but let out a loud laugh and smirk at him amusingly. "You're annoyingly funny."

"And you're annoyingly beautiful," he complimented her sweetly.

"Thank you," she whispered before wiggling her finger at him, beckoning him to come closer down to her lips. He willingly obeyed, pressing his lips to hers so that they could passionately kiss.

They talked for what felt like hours, conversing about their interests, dislikes and things they had in common. Nazariah was in love with the fact that they got along so well, and the banter between them was so natural.

They also headed back into the hotel to grab a meal together, continuing to talk and constantly kiss like any ordinary couple would do. The only thing was, they weren't a couple and Nazariah constantly being reminded of that was saddening.

But she knew she would have to deal with it. They may have been living in the same city, but Miami was one big city. He lived on one side and she lived on the other, completely different distances from each other. She knew that after this, she was most likely going to never see him again.

And she would have to deal with it.

***

"I see your sexy ass remembered my favorite color," Hassan voiced, staring lustfully at Nazariah as she stood seductively by his en-suite bathroom door. She was wearing lingerie in his favorite color, blue.

"See something you like?" she asked sexily.

"Hell yeah, I see a few things that I like," he responded cockily. "Are you just gonna stand there and keep teasing me?"

"No," she said as she turned for him, letting him see everything. From her curves, her juicy thighs, that blue thong being eaten up by her butt, her lace blue bra cupping her breasts so lovingly. Let's not forget she also had jewelry on. She had on a lacebytanaya silver crystal garter which only turned Hassan on even more. He had never seen it in person before, especially on a girl he was about to have sex with.

She slowly sauntered closer to where he was on the red king sized bed before biting her lips at him as she climbed the bed.

Once directly in front of him, Nazariah moved to sit on top of him, frontwards, so that her thighs were sitting on his lap.

He loved everything about the way she looked for him right now; even the way she smelled was heavenly. Yeah, tonight was about to be extra freaky between them. His hands began to move up and down her body, gently stroking her warm skin.

She wrapped one arm around his neck and grabbed the other one towards her right breast. The second he began to squeeze, Nazariah quietly moaned, enjoying the feel of his hand on her flesh. And she could tell he was enjoying it too, because she could feel his erection growing rapidly underneath her.

"Fuck, you know how hard you got me right now, Nazariah?" he whispered, his voice drunk with lust as he looked up at her and continued to squeeze.

She said nothing and moved to the side of his neck so that she could kiss on him, pleasing him while he pleased her.

Just when things were starting to get more heated and Nazariah could feel Hassan's free hand heading to her bra hook, a loud vibration suddenly sounded from the nearest top draw by the bed.

Zing! Zing! Zing!

"Ignore it, baby," Hassan gently instructed, unhooking her bra strap.

Nazariah nodded as she kissed her way high off Hassan's neck and onto his soft cheek, before beginning to kiss his thick, juicy lips.

While they kissed, the phone vibrations stopped and Nazariah felt herself at ease. This was the first time ever Hassan's phone had interrupted them. She prayed it was the first and last.

Slowly, Nazariah began to grind her hips hard onto Hassan's growing erection, making him groan with pleasure. She was driving him crazy. He pushed her bra up out of the way and cupped her large breasts in his palms, continuing to squeeze and stroke them.

"Hassan, that fe—"

Zing! Zing! Zing!

The vibrations had started again.

"Feels what?" he asked her, trying to ignore his phone.

"Feels so g—"

Zing! Zing! Zing!

Nazariah couldn't take it anymore. All this vibrating was irritating her soul.

She immediately reached over to open the top drawer. "Who the hell keeps on calling you right now?"

"Leave it, Nazariah," he ordered, grabbing one of her arms. "Just focus on us."

But it was too late.

Nazariah had already opened up the drawer and spotted the caller ID on his bright screen.

Wife.

Zing! Zing! Zing!

Nazariah's heart began to race with fear and just when she felt herself want to blank out and regroup her thoughts together, Hassan snapped her out of it by pulling her back closer to him.

"I told your ass to ignore i—"

"You're married?" she asked in disbelief.

Hassan immediately shut up and just sighed softly at the fact that she had seen his phone.

Yes, he was married. But what did it matter? He was with her right now and wanted to be with her only. Anybody else could fuck right off.

"Nazariah, please don't sweat about it. It's not somethin' you need to worry about," he explained, only adding fire to Nazariah's heartbroken state.

"Don't sweat about it? So you are married?"

"Yes, I am, bu—"

"But what?!" she roared, cutting him off. "You didn't think I would find out eventually? Are you fucking kidding me right now?!"

"Yo, stop with all the shoutin' in my damn face," he retorted.

"Who am I with right now? You! Stop fuckin' worrying about it, girl."

Nazariah had heard a couple seconds of his bullshit and was already done. The only thing she could think of doing was getting up out of here. Hassan was nothing but a liar, a scammer and a heartbreaker. He loved playing with her. But she was having no more of it.

Nazariah re-hooked her bra strap, quickly got off his body, slapping his hands away when he tried to keep her close to him and got out his bed.

This was all just a bunch of bullshit.

"Get your sexy ass back in this bed, Nazariah. Now."

"No."

"Come here."

Nazariah quickly shook her head no at his sudden command. She didn't want to do anything now realizing that even though he wasn't wearing a ring on his left hand, there was supposed to be one.

"I ain't gon' tell your ass again, Nazariah," he stated boldly, staring at her from where he lay. "Just come here."

"No," she whispered unconfidently, tearing her teary eyes away from his handsome face and shirtless body. "I'm leaving."

"No the fuck you ain't. A nigga hungry as fuck for you right now, and ready for you to come sit on his face all night, but now you wanna start actin' so dumb."

Without wasting another second to spare listening to him, Nazariah turned away from him and went to the glass table that she had left her silver purse on. She needed to get the hell up out of here. She couldn't allow herself to stay here with him alone. She could no longer stay up in this suite and mess around with him all night long in his bed. Allowing him to stretch her out and guide her into different positions while he slid inside her, had to stop. Allowing him to kiss and touch in private places that he had managed to gain access to, had to stop.

"Nazariah, baby, chill," he whispered gently in her left ear.

How the hell had he managed to get out of his bed so quickly and creep up behind her?

"Hassan, no. You're ma—"

"But I'm fuckin' with you right now," he said, cutting her off and pressing his large hand onto her arm. "You the one I want, Nazariah."

The way his naked body was pressing up so close and hard to hers had her heart racing. She couldn't think straight with him this close. And the way his seductive scent was filling her nostrils, she knew she was going to get drunk in love because of it.

"I don't want this, Hassan. You're married and I really don't want any problems in my life messing with you. So please let me..."

Shit.

Nazariah could feel him pressing his hard on directly on the curve of her butt. What the hell was he trying to do to her? Other than make her suffer for trying to leave him tonight.

"You don't want this?" he queried curiously, grabbing a hold of her arm and pushing her back closer to him so she was forced to stand still in front of him and feel his erection poking her ass. "You don't want this dick?"

Of course she did. She wanted every last inch of it. But it wasn't hers to want.

"Hassan, please..."

"Nah, please, what? You the one tryna leave a nigga right now. You the one worryin' about shit that don't matter right now. What matters is you and I, no one else," he explained, moving his free

106

hand in the gap between Nazariah's arm and waist, so he could place his hand on top of her flat stomach. Then, he slowly began moving his hand downwards towards the front of her blue thong.

"I've been craving that bomb ass pussy all day and now you wanna try and take it away from me? You must be crazy, girl."

She had purposely worn lingerie in his favorite color tonight, just to make him extra happy and excited.

Hassan suddenly pressed his lips against the side of her neck, quickly beginning to seduce her. He knew how weak she got from his neck kisses.

"Hassan, oh... Shit," she quietly moaned, unknowingly tilting her head to the side so that her neck was more exposed, providing him with much better access to kiss on her skin.

While he kissed, his hands went deeper past her thong and straight to her moist pussy lips.

When Nazariah felt his thick fingers beginning to play with her clit, she knew there was absolutely no going back now. He had won her once more.

"Please, Hassan..."

"Please, what?"

"Please don't," she whimpered once one of his fingers pushed inside her. "Don't do this. Don't make me want you... Even more, when I know I'm not, uhh! Supposed to."

His second finger joined in on the fun and he slowly began moving in and out of her simultaneously with both fingers.

"Shit, Hassan, please," she exclaimed out in pleasure, feeling her wetness fall down her thighs as he fingered her.

She began to rock her body against his and rode his fingers with more passion and drive. She was becoming infatuated again. She hated how weak she was around him. It wasn't fair what he did to her, knowing fully well how she would react to him. It wasn't fair at all.

"Hassan!"

"You gonna cum for me or what?" he aggressively asked, pulling her braids back with his free hand, making her head go back and resting it on his shoulder.

"No," she whispered shakily, unable to control her shaking legs as he fucked her with two fingers alone. What was he doing to her? Other than punishing her right now. She wanted to leave him but, at the same time, she wanted to stay.

"Yes you will," he ordered firmly. "Look how much I got that pussy drippin' for me already."

"It's not... I'm n... Ugh, fuuuuuuuck!" A huge gush of fluid flew out of her and all she could feel was the pleasure getting stronger and stronger. He had hit her g-spot so effortlessly and now she was squirting for him.

"Damn, now I got you squirting for me too, Nazariah," he voiced, still thrusting his two fingers in and out of her. "You definitely cummin' for me right now."

There was no way out of this tonight. Hassan wanted her and Nazariah knew he was going to have her.

MISS JENESEQUA

$ CHAPTER EIGHT $

Married.

"Nazariah, wake up, baby."

Fucking married.

"I gotta head out for my morning run, then my business meeting. I'll be back in a few hours, a'ight?"

Married to someone who wasn't her.

"I made you some breakfast. It's on the stand right next to you."

But here he was, messing around with her like they were the married ones.

"I'ma see you later, beautiful."

How could someone so fine be so deceiving and conniving? Because that's exactly what he was. If she had never looked at his phone, she never would have found out that he was married and he wouldn't have ever told her. She would have remained clueless and stupid, just like he wanted her to.

He was acting as if nothing had changed between them. As if he hadn't just dropped a bomb on her entire life and made her feel completely different about the whole entire situation. Hassan

Knight was nothing but a liar. A beautiful liar. A beautiful *married* liar.

"You can't do this anymore, Nazariah, it's time for you to leave," Nazariah explained to herself for the millionth time.

Now that Hassan had gone out for his morning run and business meeting, she knew that if she was going to have any opportunity to leave without him convincing/seducing her to stay, it was now.

How could she possibly stay?

Hassan was married. Married to a woman who knew nothing about what he was doing on vacation with her. He had played them both. His wife and his new mistress. Because that's what she was, right? His mistress.

Nazariah knew that she wasn't exactly the innocent person in this either. Her relationship with Anthony had just been recently mended and here she was, breaking it apart into tiny pieces every time she gave her body to a different man. Hassan wasn't her boyfriend. Hassan wasn't the man she had spent two years of her life being with. But why did it feel like she had known him for years? And why did he know her body so well?

He knew all the places to kiss, touch and rub. He knew how to provide her with so much pleasure without her needing to direct him. He just knew. He knew what she wanted without asking.

How could she ever forget all about him when he had been inside her so many times these past few days? Her walls would forever remember him. Him stroking deep inside her, fast, slow, however the hell she liked it.

Nazariah knew she would have to figure it out somehow, but there was absolutely no way that she was going to be able to stay in the Dominican Republic with Hassan.

She had to go.

Once coming to her final decision, Nazariah booked a quick flight back home to Miami and quickly got her things together. She hadn't unpacked much of her things into Hassan's penthouse, and it was a good thing she hadn't. He had told her to get as comfortable as she liked, but she always felt so lazy to do so.

Thank God she hadn't unpacked because trying to pack all her things back would have taken so long that she was sure that Hassan would have arrived back to his suite and caught her. Stopping her from trying to leave him.

Nazariah badly fought the urge to leave Hassan a letter or a note explaining why she was leaving. But she couldn't bring herself to do it. So she left a simple short note, letting him know that she had gone.

She did fight the urge, however, to leave a phone number or an email. As much as she wanted him, he wasn't hers for the wanting. So leaving some way for him to contact her would only lead to trouble. It was best she just parted away from him with no way of him getting in touch or finding her.

Nazariah took one last look at his beautifully modern designed penthouse, glad that she had managed to spend some time with such a fine, blessed man. But their time together was officially over. She was putting an end to this one-week stand right now.

Whatever they had been doing, was finished.

***

"What the fuck do you mean the Jamaicans lost all my shit? Who the hell do I need to kill now?"

"Boss, they were fightin' over territory with the Leones. The Leones managed to not only take over their entire operation but steal their stock, your stock."

Hassan frowned, before rubbing his hand across his forehead trying to think.

"Who the hell are these Leones anyways? Where did they

come from?" he questioned seriously.

"Atlanta, apparently. They've come to Miami to rebuild ever since being forced out by Knight Nation. Blaze's turf."

"That nigga always starting some shit," Hassan mumbled, remembering how Blaze got with that hot head of his. "Ice, you know I'm on vacation right now. Right?"

Ice quickly nodded, "Of course I do, boss."

"And I really don't want to have to start fuckin' niggas up before my vacation is even over. I hired you to oversee everything. Khyree thought you were shit from the start, but I believed in you, Ice. From the jump," Hassan explained to him. "Did I make a mistake?"

"No boss, you ain't make no mistake," Ice responded. "In fact, Khyree was the one that told me to come and tell you."

Hassan shot him a confused look. "He did?"

"Yeah and he also told me to tell you that, he's handling it."

Again, Hassan's face twisted into a confused facial expression. "If he's handling it, why couldn't he just wait 'til I got back home? Why send you all the way over here?"

"I thi—"

"Because he's stupid as fuck most times, which is why I don't usually trust him with shit like this. But hey, if he says he's handling it then I guess he is. Anything else he tell you to tell me?"

"Uh yeah… Somethin' about your wife ge—"

"Yeah, I really don't wanna hear none of that shit right about now," Hassan concluded, getting up from his seat and staring down at Ice. "Head back to Miami. Watch Khyree for me and I'll be seeing you all very soon."

"Alright, boss," Ice said obediently. "When are you coming back though?"

When was he coming back?

To be honest, Hassan wasn't sure. He wasn't sure if he was really ever coming back. Maybe the dream he had been having over and over again to stay put in the Dominican with Nazariah was going to come true. He had been having such a good time with her that he didn't want to leave. He didn't want these sweet moments with her to end. Ever.

Coming back wasn't on the table for him. He wanted to work on somehow convincing Nazariah to stay just a bit longer with him in the Dominican. Then somehow he could convince her to stay with him forever. Call him crazy, but he was willing to make it happen. She didn't need to worry about ever having to work another day in her life. He would take care of her. Anything she wanted, anything she needed, he would take care of and make sure she got it all.

Despite the fact that she had managed to find out about his marriage, Hassan wasn't taking it to heart. He hoped she wasn't either because she didn't need to worry a damn thing about his wife. She would never be an issue when it came to them; he would make sure of that without a doubt.

"I'm not sure yet, Ice. But when I do, you'll be the first to know."

***

Hassan smiled happily to himself as he flashed his card key against his lock and waited for the lock light to turn from red to green before pushing his way inside to his suite.

"Yo! Naz, baby, I'm back!"

An hour away from her and he had missed her so much. He had missed being around her. Seeing that pretty face, hearing that gentle voice and now that he was back with her, he couldn't stop smiling.

He wanted to wrap his arms around her and just romantically

rock their bodies together to the sweet sounds of Sade playing in the background, just like they had done almost every night together.

You give me the sweetest taboo

That's why I'm in love with you (with you)

You give me the sweetest taboo

Too good for me

Sometimes I think you're just too good for me

"I can't believe you have me doin' this right now Naz," he whispered calmly in her ear as she swayed with him, his strong arms wrapped around her waist as they moved together to Sade's *"The Sweetest Taboo."*

I'd do anything for you, I'd stand out in the rain

Anything you want me to do, don't let it slip away

"What? You embarrassed I got your boring ass dancing with me to Sade?" she asked with a light laugh.

"Nah, I'm shocked your slow ass can actually dance," he taunted.

There's a quiet storm

And it never felt like this before

Nazariah scoffed before responding, "You know how well I can dance. I dance for you all the time. Quit fronting like you don't know I'm the Dance Queen Champ."

"Dance Queen Champ?" he queried curiously. "Damn, I guess the Dance Queen Champ needs to give me a few private lessons."

There's a quiet storm

I think it's you

There's a quiet storm

And I never felt this hot before

Giving me something that's taboo

"Private lessons? Yeah, that'll cost you quite a lot."

"I can't get a discount?"

"Nope! You rich, ain't you? Better have my money then."

"A'ight, I'm sure I can pay you plentiful, just not with money though."

"Then how will you pay me?"

"With this big ass D," he voiced cockily. "How else?"

All Nazariah could do was laugh before turning her head around to stare at him lovingly. "You're something else you know."

"Something else that you can't resist," he commented before leaning in closer to her lips, watching her closely before locking their lips together.

Hassan quickly shook the sweet memory with him and Nazariah out of his head, suddenly remembering that Nazariah hadn't responded to his greeting when he had first entered his penthouse.

"Naz! Where you at?" he called to her, passing through his living room only to see that she was nowhere on any of the white couches.

"Nazariah!" he yelled, quickly walking to his bedroom.

He didn't like this feeling that he could feel in his heart and around him. This feeling that was telling him that something really bad had happened. Something that he wasn't going to like one bit.

"Nazariah, quit playing, girl!" he continued to shout, feeling his anger rapidly build. "Where the fuck are y…"

Just before Hassan could ask, he stepped into his bedroom only to see his red California king sized bed neatly made and Nazariah not in sight. Her suitcases had suddenly disappeared too, and the closer he sauntered into the room, the quicker he noticed how her entire vibe had left his bedroom. It felt empty, cold and lifeless. Like she had sucked the life and soul out of it and taken it to wherever the hell she was right now. Where the hell was she?!

Hassan's eyes instantly clocked onto the small yellow sticky note sitting on the middle of his bed and he walked towards it, picking it up and reading the short message on it.

I'm sorry, I just can't do this anymore. Thank you for the best four amazing nights of my life and I hope you and your wife stay happy together.

What the fuck was this bullshit?

To say Hassan was upset right now would be an understatement. A complete understatement. He was past upset. He would describe his feelings right now as completely and utterly pissed the fuck off.

He read the last few words once more. *I hope you and your wife stay happy together.*

"Fuck!" he barked, clenching his fists tightly by his sides, chucking her note to the floor and violently kicking the side of his bed.

Why would she do this?

He had developed some serious strong feelings for her over their time spent together. Just getting to know her felt wonderful. It felt refreshing and soothing to him. He hardly got to know people so getting to know her was something new to him, something that he was enjoying extremely. Then she goes ahead and leaves him?

The more Hassan deepened the situation, the angrier he became. She had exploited the fact that he had left the penthouse to plot her escape plan. She knew he wouldn't have let her leave him. He would have forced her to stay, even if he had to fuck some sense into her and make her promise to not leave him.

But his morning run and quick meeting with Ice had allowed her to leave him so easily. She had managed to slip through his fingers so quickly and smoothly.

Why did he have to leave her alone in his suite? Why didn't he have a few men guarding his door? Why didn't he have security downstairs to keep eyes on her, for him? All these fucking questions that Hassan didn't have answers to.

He had just been too dumb and way too into her, to not even think about things properly. She had just found out he was married. Of course she would still be in her feelings! Even though Hassan had tried to convince her that she had nothing to worry about,

Nazariah had still been worried.

She had probably worried all night while sleeping his arms. And he hadn't even bothered to check on her. She probably hadn't even slept all night! Just stayed up all night and thought about how she was going to leave him.

Now she had managed to do it. Leave him one stupid note, that had no phone number, no address, no email, no nothing! He didn't have one single way of getting in touch with her, and Miami was a gigantic city. It would take him months to find her, especially since he didn't even know her surname. She had never told him and he had never asked. Her finding out his just kinda slipped out since all the workers in the resort referred to him as Mr. Knight. How was he supposed to quickly find her?

But whatever the hell he had to do to get her back, he knew he was going to do it.

He originally believed that getting her to stay with him on vacation would solve the infatuation that he had with her. But it hadn't solved shit. He wanted her even more now and not just for the sex anymore. Their chemistry together was strong and Hassan truly loved it. He had loved everything about their time together and he didn't want their time to ever end.

Hassan knew that there was no way he was allowing her to

123

walk out his life like this. Not with how much time they had invested into one another. Even the fact that he was unable to one-night stand her proved a lot.

There was too much passion between them to throw away.

Hassan couldn't let her go.

$ CHAPTER NINE $

~ *A Month Later* ~

"Anthony, I'm at work right now. Can we please discuss this later?"

"What exactly do we need to discuss? I just told you my cousin is getting worse and my family wants to be together at this time. I want you with me at the dinner."

Nazariah sighed deeply once more before answering as calmly as she possibly could. "If your family wants to be together at this time, then it should just be you and your family. I don't want to impose."

"You won't be imposing, Nazariah. How could you be imposing when you're my family too?"

This is the shit he loves to say, just to get his own way, Nazariah mused.

"Anthony, I don't feel comfortable about coming along with you, that's all. I've never met any of your family and now is the time you want me to meet them? They're all going to be focusing on your cousin, then I come into the picture out of nowhere? It's not a good idea, Anthony. Let's just organize something else," Nazariah explained.

"I think it's a great idea for you to finally meet my family who have been wanting to meet you for a few months now," Anthony voiced. "No one has an issue with you coming, except you."

"Anthony, let's just discuss this later, please."

"Like I said before," he began sternly, "there's nothing to discuss. Absolutely nothing because you are coming."

"So you're forcing me to attend something that I don't want to attend? Is that what you're really doing right now?"

"Yes, I am," he snapped. "You have nothing better to do."

"How the hell did you figure that out? I might already have something planned."

"It's next Sunday, you don't go to church regularly, so like I just said, you don't have anything else better to do."

"I'm going to church."

"No you are not, Zariah," he fumed. "Stop lying."

"I'm going."

No she wasn't. As much as she believed in God, she hated church. It just wasn't for her.

"I'm going to let you think that we're discussing this later, but we really are not. You're coming with me and that's the end of discussion."

"Yeah, you know what? I think you're absolutely right, Anthony. We won't be discussing this later anymore because I'm not going, and that's the end of discussion. Bye," she concluded before hanging up the call, switching off her phone with anger and chucking it into her locker.

She heard a small snigger and looked up only to see a fully dressed into blue nurse scrubs, Amina, laughing at her. Nazariah began to mean mug her before sucking her teeth rudely as she turned back around to shut her locker.

"I'm not going and that's the end of discussion," Amina mocked Nazariah's voice in a high pitched tone. "Guuuuurl, you sure told him!" she continued to laugh.

"Quit the laughing," Nazariah ordered sulkily. "It's not funny. He thinks he's the boss of me, but he really isn't."

"He isn't?" Amina asked her in a faked shock tone. "Anthony Shawn isn't the boss of Nazariah Jordan? Houston, we have a problem."

"He isn't!" Nazariah fumed. "Yeah, we're in a relationship together but he really can't just be snapping and ordering me around on what to do. He wants me to attend some family thing that clearly sounds like it's been set up for him and his family. But still he insists that I attend. I ain't going! Like I said before, he isn't the boss of me."

"Yeah, he might not be the boss of you... But we both know exactly who the boss of Ms. Nazariah Jordan was a month ago," Amina commented smugly.

"Amina, don't," Nazariah sadly whispered.

"What? Am I lying though?"

Nazariah looked down, not wanting Amina to see how her mood had suddenly changed now that the mention of Hassan had come up.

A month later and she still wasn't over him.

Every night she closed her eyes and slept, she dreamt of him. She dreamt of those undeniably attractive green eyes, that handsome light skin face, that gorgeous, hot body, that amazing dick that had her screaming his name every time he gave it to her.

She still wasn't over him.

She couldn't even have sex anymore, certainly not with Anthony. Because every time they tried, all she could see was Hassan in her mind. Then get turned off seeing that the man on top

129

of her wasn't him.

She definitely wasn't over him one bit.

"You shouldn't have left him, Nazariah."

"He's fucking married!" she suddenly yelled, her eyes watery with tears. "What was I supposed to do? Stay with him and sing kumbaya every time I remembered that he had a wife, and act like she doesn't exist?"

"I know but… You guys really like—"

"I wasn't about to be his side chick mistress," Nazariah stated, cutting her off. "The fact that he deliberately didn't let me know just shows that we were not meant to be. It didn't matter that we liked each other, we were never going to work."

"Okay, you say all this now, but why can't you stop thinking about him? Why you always getting emotional when I bring him up?"

"Because I was falling for him. Badly," she responded truthfully. "And I'm trying my hardest every single day to forget all about him. I don't want to want him anymore. I just want to go back to being normal Nazariah, with no feelings for him whatsoever."

"I think that the fact that you left without at least talking to him

130

about how you truly felt about him being married, made it worse," Amina explained. "You see, with Khyree and I, we didn't necessarily talk about us but we still talked. And when he didn't ask me to stay I just knew that that was his way of saying that there wasn't nothing for us."

"He didn't even ask you for your number?"

"Oh he did," Amina answered simply. "I just gave him a fake one."

"What? You gave him a fake one? You never told me this."

"You never asked," Amina voiced. "Besides, he wasn't interested in me."

"Yes he was! What do you me—"

"He just wanted to smash, Nazariah, that's all he wanted from the jump. See, the difference between him and Hassan is that, Hassan smashed you and still wanted more of you. Khyree just wanted to smash so he could add me onto his I hit it list. I know the way these guys operate, and I could smell it from the jump but I just played along. At first I thought that because I was developing small feelings for him that something could grow between us, but I thought wrong. Absolutely wrong."

"Are you sure that all he wanted from you was sex, Amina?"

Nazariah asked with a perfectly arched brow up in the air.

"Positive," she said. "Nothing was going to happen between us. So it's good I gave him a fake number. Besides, if I had given him the real one I know for a fact that he would have given it to Hassan. And Hassan would be blowing up my phone so much."

"What? Why?"

"To get to you," Amina explained. "I guarantee you, he's been looking for you."

"Looking for me?" Nazariah asked.

"Yes, Nazariah," she insisted. "Looking for you. You left him with nothing but sweet moments. No number, no address and you think he's just gonna let you go?"

"It's been a month now and he's not here. I think he got the message."

"Or he's just been struggling to find you. We both know how big Miami is."

"If he was really looking for me, which he's not, he would have found me," Nazariah replied.

"You told him you live in downtown Miami, right?"

Nazariah slowly nodded.

132

"You know how many people live in downtown Miami?"

Nazariah just shrugged before concluding, "He's not and he shouldn't be. He's married and he should just focus on his marriage and leave me the hell alone."

But leaving her alone was exactly what he had been doing.

***

"So you found out where she works and you haven't run up in there already? Damn, bro, I'm actually quite shocked," Khyree commented honestly, watching as Hassan took a quick puff of his Cuban cigar before placing it back onto its holder.

He knew that his brother hated cigars, so to see him smoke it now only meant one thing. He was stressed.

"I don't want to make her feel uncomfortable."

"Huh?"

"She left because she was uncomfortable."

Khyree shot him an amused look. "You didn't care why she left, a month ago you were desperate to get her back."

"And now I'm not."

"Why? You're suddenly magically over her?" he asked Hassan

curiously.

"She left because she was uncomfortable with me being married. She was hurt and probably still is. So I'll leave her be," Hassan announced.

"You damn mothafucking liar," Khyree voiced with a smirk. "There's no way you're leaving her after all that trouble you put your P.I. through, to get that address. You still like her."

"And you still get on my damn nerves," Hassan retorted. "But there's nothing we can do about either of those two things."

"So you ain't going to go see her?"

Hassan looked away from Khyree's gaze and stared down at his bright phone screen in his left hand.

Jackson Memorial Hospital

1611 NW 12th Ave

Miami

FL 33136

United States

The address of where she worked, in his hands right now and ready for him to go to whenever he desired.

Truth was, since he had been back in Miami and desperately looking for Nazariah, she was the only thing on his mind. Not only had he been stressing his private investigator out in finding her, he had also been stressing himself out.

He had constantly been pondering why things had turned out all pear shaped between them and the more he thought about why Nazariah had left him, the more he understood. The more he understood, the more he started to feel bad.

Now knowing where she worked was supposed to make him feel over the moon for finally being able to know a location she was constantly at, but it only gave him cold feet.

He was nervous to see her.

And he just didn't understand why. He wasn't usually nervous and he had never been nervous over any girl before, but Nazariah wasn't any girl, anymore. She had become someone completely different. She was the only woman that had ever made butterflies fly in his stomach when he thought about her. They hadn't seen each other in a month and she was still having such an effect on him.

"Just go and see her, Hassan. You've been waiting for this for a whole month. Now you backin' out like a little punk?"

She had turned him into a little punk.

"First of all, fool," Hassan coldly began, "I ain't no punk. The real punk here is you, using me to get to somehow see Amina again."

"Is it my fault she gave me a fake number?"

"Yes, because you should have just asked her to stay," Hassan advised.

"I didn't think she would say yes!" he protested, raising his arms up in the air.

"Well you had your chance and blew it."

"But you still have a chance with Nazariah."

"She doesn't want me, Ky," he sadly reminded him. "Especially since I'm married."

"Get out of your marriage then," Khyree casually said, making Hassan shoot him a rude stare. "Okay… Then go and talk to Nazariah. Talk things out with her."

"I don't think she's gonna want to listen. And easy as it is for me to make her listen, I don't want to force her to. Not right now."

"All these fuckin' excuses, nigga." Khyree waved him off. "Just admit that you're scared. You scared to see her."

"Shut up, I'm not."

"You are," Khyree pushed. "For the first time in his life, Hassan Knight is scared and nervous."

"Think what you want, but I'm not gon' make her feel uncomfortable anymore. I only want what's best for her. If that means not bein' with me, then so be it."

Who was he trying to kid?

Hassan knew damn well that Nazariah was the woman he wanted. She was the only woman that he wanted.

It was just these damn nerves. These damn nerves that he didn't like feeling all the time he thought of going to see her.

They needed to go away because he just wasn't sure he could deal with them.

***

"I'm going out."

"I know, Hassan," she replied with a happy smile. "That's why I got dressed."

Hassan turned around to look at her only to see her fully dressed in a long black maxi dress like they were about to head out together.

"Do me a favor real quick. You see that wardrobe you're in front of? Open it and go look for something for me," he instructed her coolly.

Dominique simply obeyed and opened the mahogany wardrobe, taking a peek inside. "Alright, baby, but what exactly am I looking for right now?"

"You lookin' inside the wardrobe, right? It should be in there."

Dominique stared into the wardrobe only seeing her clothes neatly hanging up. "I'm looking, Hassan, but I still don't know what you're looking for?"

"Your damn motherfucking mind," he spat angrily. "Because clearly you've lost it. That's why you actin' so dumb right now."

Dominique could feel her blood begin to boil as she listened to Hassan insult her.

"You said you're going out and I'm telling you that I'm dressed," she voiced, shutting the wardrobe. "I want to come with you, Hassan. As your wife, what's the harm in coming out with you?"

"Did I say you could come out with me?"

"No, bu—"

"So why the hell did you come up with a stupid idea of getting dressed and coming with me? Clearly something isn't working correctly in that head of yours."

"All I wanted to do was spend some time with you," she whispered. "We haven't spent much time together in months. It's been worse since you came back from the Dominican..."

Hassan took a deep breath, trying to remain calm and cool.

"Dominique, go get some rest. You should be in bed."

"But I don't want to sleep, Hassan, I want to go out with you!"

"And who the hell are you raising your voice at like that?" he firmly questioned her.

"You, nigga," she barked. "I'm fully capable of doing that."

"Oh, so you're fully capable of doing that? Are you fully capable of gainin' some common sense and going to bed?"

"I just told you that I don't want to go to bed, Hassan!"

"Dominique, I ain't gon' ask you again," he snapped, turning away from her to head to the door. He needed to leave. An important meeting had just popped up and he couldn't miss it. "Get to bed."

"Alright... Alright..." He could hear how tired she was in her voice. She shouldn't have tried arguing with him. She was only hurting herself. "But Hassan, there's something… There's something I need to ask you… Something I need to know."

Hassan slowly turned around only to see that her dress was off, revealing her skinny naked body and her wig was off, revealing her bald skin head.

"Are you cheating on me?"

Loving My Miami Boss

$ CHAPTER TEN $

"Tell me one more time what happened, Kingsley," Hassan simply ordered.

"You wan' me to talk when yah rassclart broda got a gun to me head?" Kingsley asked in his thick Jamaican accent while staring from Hassan to Khyree.

"If your stupid ass actually did what you were supposed to do and not let our product get stolen, this wouldn't be a problem, now would it?" Khyree continued, pressing his black pistol to the side of Kingsley's dark forehead.

"Kingsley," Hassan gently called him before giving him a small smile. "Just tell me."

"We've been beefin' wit' da Leones over territory for a minute now. Dey finally made a big hit on our stuff and took it all."

"And you all couldn't stop them?"

"We tried to, but seein' that dem niggas had AK-47s and grenades, tings we don't have wit us at that trap house, we fled."

"You fled," Hassan stated coolly with a light sigh.

"Yas, boss."

"You fled, allowing them niggas to take all the shit that you

142

were supposed to protect with your life, Kingsley," Hassan commented through gritted teeth.

"Wat were we 'posed to do man? Let them kill us all?"

"We've constantly given you ammo to protect yourselves over the years, Kingsley," announced Khyree. "You mean to tell me you didn't have a single thing to defend yourselves that night?"

Hassan could smell a rat.

The more he thought about the situation with the Jamaicans and Leones, the more he began to feel strange about the whole entire thing. How had the ruthless Jamaicans just allowed some random ass cats come around and jack all their shit?

Something didn't feel right. Someone was fucking around him and he wasn't liking it one bit.

"We were unprepared. Dose fools caught us completely off guard, that's all. I promise yah it won't happen again," Kingsley promised.

"Damn right it won't happen again," Khyree snapped, lifting his gun off Kingsley's head. "Because the next time you and your boys allow some shit like this to happen again, let's just say you won't be sittin' here comfortably to tell us the tale."

Kingsley nodded, understanding Khyree's words before

speaking. "It won't happen again."

Hassan kept silent and just continued to glare at Kingsley. Whether or not he was lying, Hassan was sure that all would be revealed to him very soon. One thing he couldn't stand was niggas trying to play him, his business and his money.

And he prayed to God that the Jamaicans weren't playing him. Because if they were, Hassan was going to make sure it a deadly day for them all.

"Something isn't sitting right with me, San," Khyree voiced with a frown. Now that Kingsley had left Hassan's office, he could freely speak his thoughts to his brother. "I think they're stealing from us."

"I hope to God they ain't," Hassan responded.

"And if they are, what are we going to do about it?"

"We'll decide when we know for sure," Hassan explained. "For now, we watch them closely and pay attention. Any next wrong move they make, we'll be the ones catching them out before they even realize it."

Khyree nodded in agreement before getting up from his seat opposite Hassan. "I'ma see you later, bro... Matter fact, Sunday, right?"

"Sunday," Hassan nonchalantly stated.

He wasn't looking forward to Sunday one bit. And it was because of Dominique and what she had been so determined to make sure that he came to. But even still, he knew there was a very strong chance that he wasn't attending.

Dominique Knight.

Hassan's wife of two years, going on three this Sunday. The one person that had managed to drive Nazariah away without them even meeting each other first.

Dominique was someone who Hassan had fallen in love with so fast and so naturally. He thought she was perfect. She did everything he wanted, without even needing to ask him. She just knew. She listened to him, she treated him right, she cooked, she cleaned, and she showered with him with all the love and affection he ever could need.

But Dominique seeming perfect had all been a lie. Just one big lie because with her perfect persona came with secrets. Secrets that became so twisted and deep into Dominique's life that it drove Hassan crazy. It got to the point that her real name wasn't even Dominique but because of who was looking for her now, she couldn't go back to her real identity. Not even back to the other twenty five identities that she had created during the course of her life.

She was what one would call a scammer. She scammed whoever she could and whenever she could, for their money, cars, houses and whatever else she could get her hands on. She was supposed to scam Hassan but she had fallen in love with him, she claimed, and she couldn't bring herself to steal from him.

When he first found out the truth about her, he wanted to leave her. But she knew too much. She knew all about who he was, what he did and he feared that he would constantly have to worry about her snitching to the Feds out of revenge for him leaving her.

Dominique was fully aware of who Hassan was and what he did in Miami with his brother, Khyree. Him and Khyree were the main distributors of the entire coast of Miami, providing mostly all of the drug cartels in Miami with drugs to sell and make a profit with.

But then, he figured because she was fully aware of who he was, she knew exactly what he was capable of. So she couldn't dare try snitch. However, the day he told her it was over between them, Dominique dropped a bomb.

She had cancer.

Pancreatic cancer in fact. And when heading to the hospital

with her, to make sure she wasn't lying, the doctor told him exactly what he didn't want to hear. Dominique was in stage four pancreatic cancer and the cancer had spread to her liver.

She had less than three to six months left to live.

Finding that out made Hassan not only feel pity for her but guilt that he had tried to leave her. There was no way that he could leave her while she was going through this. It would only make her condition even worse than it was already. And the small family that she had, her cousin, auntie and uncle, would only look down at Hassan like he was a monster.

She didn't have her mom or dad who could actually be there for her. Hassan was the only person, and he couldn't just throw away all the love that he used to have for her a very long time ago. He had to stand by her until it was her time to go.

Despite Dominique being in stage four cancer and constantly going through treatment, which was weakening her energy every day, she was determined to live the rest of her life like a normal, healthy person would. She declined staying full time in the hospital to receive her chemotherapy.

Hassan wasn't about to force her into doing something that she clearly didn't want to do. So he let her do whatever she wanted, and he continued to look after her by paying for everything she wanted.

That's why he had told Nazariah that she didn't need to sweat about his wife. He was no longer in love with her and quite frankly, he was only still with her because she didn't have anyone else who could support her like he did.

If only he had had the chance to properly explain the situation to Nazariah, then maybe she wouldn't have left him and she wouldn't have gotten so worked up over nothing.

There was no point in her worrying when he only wanted her. But still, his cold feet were holding him back from going to go get her.

Was wanting her really the right thing for him, right now?

***

Nazariah looked down at her half empty plate of food before digging her fork back into her lasagna.

The silence was becoming unbearable.

She would honestly leave if this is how awkward things were going to be between them. He wasn't even striking up conversation, asking her how her day had gone like he always did.

He was just doing this on purpose, because she had told him

that she wasn't attending his family get together. She wasn't joking; her attending wasn't happening.

He couldn't force her to do a damn thing that she didn't want to do.

"So you're just going to sit there and not address the bullshit you told me over the phone?"

Ha! Finally, he speaks.

Nazariah looked up from her plate with her face twisted into a displeased facial expression. Anthony had finally broken his silence.

"The bullshit?" she questioned him with a stern face. "The bullshit that was nothing but facts you mean?"

"Yes, the bullshit," he snapped, dropping his fork loudly against his plate. "You can't seriously be considering going against something I want. Something I want for the both of us."

"Something that you want for only you, Anthony," Nazariah voiced. "This isn't about us. This is about you wanting to look high and mighty in front of your family. Despite the stuff that's going on with you all, you still want to be the center of attention."

"That's what you believe? You believe I'm doing this for some damn attention?"

Nazariah nodded stiffly. "I strongly do."

"I'm doing this because I want my family to meet my girlfriend, who they want to meet."

"We just got back together over two months ago, Anthony," Nazariah reminded him. "And you're already back to your controlling ways."

"I'm not trying to control you, Nazariah. Stop making this into something it isn't."

"How are you not controlling me by telling me what I'm going to? Even though I've told you over 10 times that I'm not going."

"Alright," Anthony said with a sigh. "You're not going."

Finally, he was understanding Nazariah's words, and she happily tucked back into the rest of her meal, pleased that Anthony wasn't dragging this situation on any further.

But as she began to eat again, she noticed Anthony's sad facial expression and the way he slowly twirled his fork across his plate.

Now she felt like shit.

Guilt immediately overcame her once she realized how much of a rubbish girlfriend she was being. If she wasn't willing to support him, then why was she with him? If she wasn't going to stand by him, then there was no point of this relationship.

"Anthony, look... I'm sorry," she announced gently, staring at him carefully.

"No, don't be," he responded. "I love you too much for you to be unhappy. I don't want you to feel uncomfortable doing anything you don't want to do. I mean, I would love you to meet my family but if it's not the right time, then I guess it isn't the right time."

What was Nazariah's actual reason for not wanting to meet Anthony's family? The more she thought about the question, the more she realized she had no real reason. She was just being selfish and stubborn.

"Anthony, baby, actually..."

She was going and he knew it too.

MISS JENESEQUA

$ CHAPTER ELEVEN $

"Guys, I want you all to meet my amazing girlfriend," Anthony gladly announced with a smile. "...Nazariah."

"Hello," Nazariah greeted them all warmly, shooting them a wave as she stared at them all.

Anthony's family was far more welcoming than she had expected. And seeing them so pleased and grateful to see her had her happy and slightly annoyed with herself for not wanting to meet them all in the first place. It was just his mom, father and cousin. His cousin who was currently going through cancer.

"So delighted to have you here with us," Anthony's mom, Elizabeth stated before pulling her in for a hug.

"And it's good to know Anthony's finally found someone to tolerate him," Anthony's cousin commented amusingly. "I'm Dominique, Anthony's favorite cousin."

"That's what she loves to believe but she's really my only cousin. So I'm forced to put up with her," Anthony joked.

Nazariah smiled as she took a good look at Dominique. For someone who had cancer, she looked surprisingly good. She was skinny, yes, but her face still held so much color and health. She still looked fashionable with a full face of makeup and clad in a

153

light pink jumpsuit with white Louboutins on her feet.

She was a light-skinned woman, standing at 5'4", with brown eyes, full lips, and a medium sized nose. She wore a full length of dark brown hair that Nazariah was sure of being a wig.

"It's so nice to finally meet you," Nazariah said calmly.

"Should we head in?" Anthony's dad, Curtis, queried.

The five of them were all standing outside a family restaurant called *Pier 94*.

"Yeah, let's do that," Dominique agreed before leading the way to the front entrance.

They arrived inside to the beautifully decorated restaurant, with white roses neatly placed up on the ivory walls.

"Table for seven," Dominique told the waiter. "Two more people are running a bit late."

"Okay, no problem," the waiter said before he led them all to a free table.

Nazariah was slightly intrigued by the fact that two people were yet to arrive. Anthony hadn't mentioned anything to her about them. She figured she would just have to wait 'til they arrived for her to see them.

"So Nazariah, Anthony told us that you're a nurse?" They had just gotten settled at their table and the conversation between them all was starting to flow again.

Nazariah instantly nodded at Anthony's mom enthusiastically. "Yes, I am."

"And you like it?"

"I love it," she replied honestly. "It's the only job I could ever see myself doing."

"That's good, that's good," Elizabeth stated.

"Is being a nurse stressful?" Dominique questioned curiously.

"Umm... At times it can be, but it's not bad stress for me. I think a little bit of stress can be a good thing, you know? Keeps things interesting."

"Definitely." Dominique nodded. "How long have you been a nurse for?"

"Two years now," Nazariah informed her. "It's been pretty fun, so I hardly feel the years. I guess because I love it so much, it doesn't actually feel like a jo—"

"Baby, you're finally here!" Dominique suddenly shouted with so much excitement and joy before getting up out her seat.

Nazariah couldn't help but smile at how her mood had turned even more positive. She wondered who had suddenly arrived that had Dominique feeling so happy.

Nazariah had her back facing the door so she couldn't see who had entered, but nonetheless she got up out her seat, seeing that Anthony and his family had done the same.

"You're about to meet Dominique's husband and his brother," Anthony informed her in a low whisper before grabbing hold of her hand. "They're cool people. Stinking rich too."

Nazariah slowly nodded as they both turned around to face Dominique hugging on her husband. Her husband who looked strangely like…

Shit.

"Hassan, Khyree, so nice of you to finally join us," Curtis announced proudly.

No, no, no.

This couldn't be happening right now. Nazariah wanted to be swallowed up by the ground right about now. She wanted to be anywhere but here. Any other place but here.

Hassan hadn't noticed her because when he had first stepped into the restaurant, her head was towards him. And she had

156

changed her hair from the last time he had seen her. But he had definitely noticed her now. Her hair was no longer braided but instead, it was long and silky straight.

What the fuck was she doing here?

She still looked as beautiful as the first time he had ever laid eyes on her. Seeing her now had him feeling all types of emotions. From confusion, happiness to jealousy. Jealousy because of the man she was holding hands with. The man that he knew as Dominique's cousin. They were together?

Once Dominique's cousin spoke up, his jealousy heightened. "Hassan, Khyree, this is my girlfriend... Nazariah."

Neither Hassan nor Khyree could speak. They were too shocked, especially Hassan. He honestly couldn't believe this was happening right now. Was Nazariah really standing in the same room as him right now? Or was this a nightmare that he needed to wake up from, as soon as possible?

"Is something wrong?" Dominque questioned them all. "You all look like you've seen a ghost."

Hassan definitely felt like he was staring at a ghost. A beautiful ghost that had deceived him. She had failed to tell him that she had a relationship also waiting for her when she got back home.

She was a beautiful liar.

Nazariah quickly shook her head no before voicing, "It's nice to meet you both."

"Likewise," Khyree responded quietly, staring at her with an intense gaze.

Hassan, on the other hand, couldn't speak. He was still in so much shock. He couldn't even comprehend what was going on properly.

Nazariah, the girl that he had fallen for over a month ago, was in a relationship with his sick wife's cousin. This was all becoming a bit too much.

"Excuse me for a minute, I need some air," Hassan explained to them all, before turning on his heels and leaving.

Khyree swiftly followed behind him and seeing that he was heading back towards his Lamborghini, he called out to him.

"Hassan! Wait up, man!"

Hassan ignored him and continued walking to his car, determined to leave. He wasn't sure he had the willpower to do this.

"Hassan!" Khyree yelled. "What the hell are you doing?"

Hassan turned around to face Khyree who was now running towards him. "Leavin'. What else would I be doing?"

"You're leaving because of her?" he asked in disbelief.

"I can't do this," he spat. "I can't sit there and play happy families, with Dominique sitting next to me and the girl I can't stop thinking about sitting opposite me with another nigga."

"And how you think she feels seeing you and Dominique together?"

"She doesn't give a sh—"

Khyree cut him off. "You saw the look on her face, man! She still has feelings for you."

Hassan rubbed a hand across his face, feeling his frustrations and stress as he played over the scene of seeing Nazariah standing next to Anthony, over and over again.

"Don't go man. You can do this," Khyree advised. "You need to do this."

Hassan took a deep breath, trying to remain as calm as he possibly could. Khyree was right, he needed to do this. What was the point of running away like a little bitch? It wasn't in his nature to ever run away from situations, but seeing Nazariah tonight had made him want to run away. Something no female ever made him

159

do.

So Hassan went back inside, acted like nothing was wrong, and introduced himself to Nazariah like he hadn't had his mouth on her pussy over a month ago. He acted like he had never seen her before in his life and just tried his best to remain cool, as if this whole thing wasn't making his mind go crazy.

Nazariah on the other hand, couldn't take it. She couldn't take the fact that the Knight Brothers were sitting opposite her and watching her, knowing fully well who she was but acting as if they hadn't. They were acting so natural, eating, drinking and conversing when they felt like it.

The more those green eyes looked at her, the more she felt like she was about to lose her mind. It didn't matter how many times she tried to avoid his gaze, she always found their eyes locking once more.

The man that she had slept with for four days in the Dominican Republic was at the same dinner as her. With his wife *and* her boyfriend.

Now Hassan's words about his wife not being an issue were starting to make sense. Because of her cancer, he didn't see her as a problem. That only angered Nazariah further. How could she not sweat about someone who clearly loved him, just because she was sick?

Nazariah could see the way Dominique constantly looked at him. She was madly in love with him and whether he felt the same or not, it wasn't right. It wasn't right that Nazariah had messed around with him.

The guilt that she had tried so hard to bury deep inside her, had grown back again and now knowing that Anthony and Hassan were cousins-in-law, only made the guilt even worse. Hassan Knight was going to remain a part of her life if she chose to stay with Anthony.

Hassan Knight was *forever* going to be a part of her life if she stayed with Anthony…

MISS JENESEQUA

$ CHAPTER TWELVE $

Nazariah slowly walked across her apartment corridor, trying to get to her room but also constantly replaying her crazy night in her head.

Had that all just really happened?

Had Hassan Knight, the man she had met on vacation last month, sat opposite her for three whole hours and pretended like he had never met her before? Was he really married to Anthony's cousin?

Nazariah couldn't even process the whole night properly. It still felt like a dream. Only this dream she couldn't wake up from. She was forced to face it.

What she really needed right now was a nice, soothing bath and then a good night's sleep. Tomorrow she had work but that wasn't about to stop her from trying to relax after tonight.

As much as she wanted to call Amina and let her know immediately what had gone down tonight, she knew how tired she would be right now and getting ready for bed. It was 10:30 p.m., so she would just have to speak to her tomorrow at work and fill her in on everything.

Nazariah sighed as she began to strip off each article of her clothing, one by one. Her eyes gently shut as she tried to remain as peaceful and calm as she possibly could. But it didn't help. All she could see and think about was him.

Why the hell had she allowed herself to get so deeply involved with him in the Dominican? This was honestly her fault for allowing him to get so close to her and have access to her cookie so quickly. She was dealing with the consequences of her actions.

After her bath, Nazariah dried herself, creamed herself with her favorite strawberry lotion, and put on her white lace dressing gown. Then she headed straight to bed, trying her hardest to fall asleep without thinking about him.

But that was easier said than done, especially since she couldn't sleep and Hassan was the only person on her mind.

What had he done to her?

All she found herself doing was constantly shuffling in her bed, tossing and turning and still restless. Sleep clearly wasn't coming to her anytime soon and it only became worse when she imagined loud knocks sounding on her front door.

Now, not only could she not fall asleep, she was hearing things.

Knock! Knock! Knock!

Nazariah instantly sat up straight in her bed, taking a quick

164

peak at her clock to see the time at 11:45 p.m.

Those knocks didn't sound imaginary at all. They sounded real, as if someone was really knocking on her door right now.

Knock! Knock! Knock!

Someone really was knocking on her door. But who? Nazariah never expected anyone to come around, except Amina, Anthony or her mother. But they usually called before they came around, so it couldn't have been any one of them at the door right now.

Knock! Knock! Knock!

Nazariah was forced to get up and leave her bed, before walking out her bedroom, past her kitchen and living room and straight to her front door.

One look through her door hole and she found herself almost gasping with fear.

What. The. Hell?

"Open up the door, Nazariah," he firmly announced. "I know you're there."

Nazariah only stepped far away from her dark brown door and felt her breathing increase rapidly.

What was he doing here? How had he even found out where

she was staying? He must have followed her home.

He still looked so damn attractive from dinner tonight, wearing a black shirt, black jeans and black Giuseppe's leather mid-tops on his feet. Two gold chains were peeking out from his shirt, gold studs clasped in each ear, and a gold Versace watch on his wrist.

"Nazariah, open the door," he ordered once more. "We need to talk."

"I'm not opening the door," she managed to make out nervously. "So just go."

"You ain't openin' the door? After I just told you to?"

The fact that he believed that he was the boss of her almost made Nazariah want to laugh. Almost.

"A'ight, that's absolutely fine," he stated coolly. "You don't need to open the door for me at all."

Satisfied that he had gotten the message and was going to leave, Nazariah turned away from her door, heading back to her bedroom, until she heard the sound of her lock being turned. It was as if someone was about to enter her apartment.

"Hassan, don't you dare!" she protested, suddenly angry with what he was doing.

"You the one that doesn't want to let a nigga in," he snapped, still picking away at her lock. "I ain't fuckin' leaving."

Just when he could feel his bobby pin hitting the correct spot, a lock suddenly unlocked and the door was swung open in front of him.

He looked up from where he was on his knees, only to look up in awe at her gorgeous face being revealed to him once more.

"Five minutes," she sternly said, leaving her door open as she entered back inside.

All Hassan could do was keep a straight face as he watched her walk in nothing but her lace dressing gown. Her dressing gown that fit so lovingly and perfectly around her body. Her body that he had missed touching so much.

Nazariah took a seat on her brown love seat, crossing her arms across her chest and staring into the space ahead of her. She waited for him to close her door and come towards the empty seat near her.

Silence suddenly hit them both and all Nazariah could do was continue to avoid eye contact with him, hoping that he would speak up and say what the hell he needed to, then go.

"The best four amazing nights of your life," Hassan spoke up, his voice full of optimism.

Nazariah refused to look at him but was still intrigued. "What?"

"You don't remember that shit?" he asked, staring at her as she stared somewhere else. "On the note you left me."

She said nothing. Of course she remembered. How on earth could she forget?

"The note you left me on the morning you decided to run away," he retorted, becoming frustrated that she wasn't looking at him. "Not even giving me a chance to explain shit... Look at me, Nazariah!"

Her head snapped in his direction, and the fear of staring at that handsome face quickly built again.

"Why the fuck did you leave me? I told you that you didn't need t—"

She cut him off. "I didn't need to worry about your cancer diagnosed wife? Is that what you meant?"

"I told you that you didn't need to sweat about her, but still you let her get under your skin," he explained. "Yes, we're married, but I don't love her, Nazariah."

"But she loves you," she replied.

"And I'm guessing you love that nigga, Anthony, the way he loves you?"

Nazariah, guilty, looked away from him again. She didn't love Anthony. Sure, she liked him, but love? That wasn't on the table for them.

"You weren't the innocent one in the situation either, so please don't act like you were. You over here judging me for havin' a wife but all the while you had a fuckin' boyfriend!"

"But I'm not married!" she yelled. "That's the difference between you and I, I'm not married. You are. You say you don't love your wife, then why the hell are you still with her?"

"Because she's sick, Naz," he quietly explained. "I can't leave her, not now that she's in her final stages. I'm not that kind of person."

"Well, it's nice to see you have some type of heart, but clearly not enough for you to freely cheat on her. I bet I'm not the only woman you had sex with that vacation."

"Look, before I met you, I really didn't give a shit about anyone's feelings or anything like that," he admitted. "Yeah, I slept with some other girls but that was way before you. When I

169

first saw you, I pictured us sleeping together and never seein' each other again. But I couldn't bring myself to do it, Naz… I couldn't one-night stand you because I had fallen for you."

"I wish I could say the same," she lied.

"What?"

"I said, I wish I could say the same! But I won't!" she exclaimed. "I can't fall for idiots like you, who deceive me about their marriage, put me in awkward situations, and stalk me all the way home."

"How the fuck have I put you in an awkward situation? How was I supposed to know that I was goin' to see your ass tonight, Nazariah?" he voiced firmly. "How the fuck was I supposed to know that shit?!"

"I have no idea who the hell you think you're yelling at rig—"

"Don't fuckin' play with me right now, Nazariah," Hassan fumed, with a crazy look in his green eyes. "You gon' end up getting yourself in trouble now."

Nazariah shot him an unimpressed look with a raised brow. "Trouble? You must be crazy."

"Crazy?" he queried with a devilish smile. "You haven't seen crazy yet, girl."

"Sure have! Because that's exactly what you are. Only a crazy fool uses a bobby pin to pick my lock because I refuse to let him into *my* apartment."

"Shut the fuck up," he ordered.

"Make me," she challenged confidently, keeping a stern face as she looked at him sitting across from her.

Just hearing her challenging him, had Hassan in his feelings again. Even the annoying shit she did turned him on. He had missed this. Their little arguments because of that fast, smart mouth of hers. He had missed her.

"Now, if you're done with your storytelling for the night, I suggest you leave my apartment and head back home to your wife," Nazariah instructed calmly.

"I ain't goin' nowhere."

Nazariah was sure that she hadn't heard correctly. "Huh?"

"You heard me," he affirmed. "I ain't goin'."

"Why the hell not?"

"Because I want to stay."

"I don't want you here, Hassan!" she cried. "Leave!"

Hassan simply sighed before sinking himself further back into Nazariah's couch, getting as comfortable as he possibly could. He was dead ass serious about not leaving. He hadn't seen her in over a month and now she expected him to just leave? She was the crazy one.

Nazariah watched him relax onto her sofa, with annoyance and her frustrations mounting. Why was he doing this? Did he not know the effect he had on her? How he knew how to drive her insane but also make her wet at the same damn time?

"What do you want from me?" she asked in a low voice. She honestly wanted to know. There had to be some reason for him doing all this.

"You said you wish you could say the same about fallin' for me," he reminded her. "You really mean that shit?"

"And if I did?"

"Answer my damn question, Nazariah, and stop tryna be so smart all the time," he retorted. "Did you mean it?"

"No," she sheepishly answered. "No, I didn't."

"So…?"

"So what?"

"Stop actin' dumb, Naz, like you don't know what the hell I'm tryna find out from you," he snapped.

"Well, if you stop beating around the bush like a damn coward, then maybe you can find out what it is you want."

Hassan gave her a dirty look, before shaking his head at her and deciding to keep quiet. Her and that smart mouth of hers was forever going to be a problem, unless he did something about it.

"Yes, Hassan," she announced with a soft sigh. "I've fallen for you."

He hadn't expected himself to light up with so much happiness inside after hearing her say those words. He wasn't even expecting it at this rate, with the way she was acting so stubborn, but hearing her say it now was truly heaven on earth for him.

"What did you just say?"

"You heard me, Hassan."

"Say it again," he demanded.

Nazariah was quickly reminded of how much Hassan loved getting his own way. "I don't want to say it again because someone's getting a little too gassed up now."

Hassan slowly got up out his seat and walked to the loveseat

Nazariah was cozily sitting on by herself. Seeing him get up had her nerves suddenly flying through the roof. Hassan already being in her apartment was driving her crazy, but now that he was coming to sit next to her, how was she supposed to think straight?

The second his body was positioned on the seat close to hers, Nazariah felt butterflies flying in her stomach. Just like when she had felt butterflies this evening when she had laid eyes on him once more.

"Say it again," Hassan ordered, leaning in close to her face and watching her.

Nazariah simply shook her head 'no', unable to properly to speak with how close Hassan was and how close he was getting to her lips. All she could do was stare helplessly into those mesmerizing green eyes of his.

"Please, Naz," he pleaded in a whisper, grabbing a hold of the side of her face and gently stroking her soft skin.

She continued to shake her head 'no' and just looked at him, feeling the sexual tension between them grow rapidly.

"You ain't gonna give me what I want?" he firmly asked, eyeing her through hooded eyes.

"You don't need to hear me say it again, Hassan. It doesn't

matter whether or not I've fallen for you," she commented. "We can't be together."

"We've already been together," he said. "Over and over again, we've been together. I've had you in positions and doin' shit that he could never get you to do. I've made love to you and made you cum in ways he could never…"

Nazariah's heart began to race faster and faster the more she heard Hassan's deep, sexy baritone whisper to her. He just didn't know what he was doing to her. Or maybe he did know and he just wanted to have her feeling like this.

"Just tell me and I promise you I'll do what you want."

"And what is it that I want?"

"For me to leave, right?" Hassan asked.

Nazariah wasn't sure now. Originally, that's what she wanted, but now her heart wanted something completely different. Her heart wanted him. What the hell had he done to her to make her change her mind so fast?

He has a wife, Nazariah. You have a boyfriend. This isn't going to work. You won't be able to do this.

But even with her troubling thoughts, Nazariah knew exactly what she wanted. Who she wanted.

Instead of telling him what he wanted to hear, Nazariah got up, took Hassan by the hand, and led him straight to her bedroom.

Once inside, she slowly helped him undress, not bothering to explain herself on what she was doing. She just unbuttoned his shirt, removed it off his body, and chucked it to the side. Finding it awfully hard to tear her eyes away from that chiseled, hot body of his.

Then, she pulled him into her bed and laid right next to him, still remaining quiet.

Hassan figured she no longer wanted to talk and would rather just let her actions do the speaking. From her actions, he got the sense that she wanted him. But not for the sex tonight, just for the company. His company. And he was gladly going to give it to her.

"Lose the gown, Naz," he announced, looking down at her.

"W-what, why?"

"Just lose it," he reiterated. "I promise I won't try anything."

Nazariah simply exhaled before doing as he asked, and removed her lace gown. Now she was in nothing but her black lace panties, and even though Hassan had already seen her naked many times before, this time around she was nervous.

"Turn around."

She had her back towards him and Hassan didn't like it. He wanted to be able to admire her beautiful body before they fell asleep, knowing that she now belonged to him. Because there was no way after this he was letting her go. They belonged to each other from now on.

Nazariah slowly turned around shyly, avoiding Hassan's hard gaze by staring down at his hard chest. But when she felt her chin being tugged up, she knew there was no escaping him now.

"I know shit is complicated right now, Nazariah, but I want to be with you," he sweetly whispered. "I want us to be together and despite what you may think about me, I'm a good guy. Well... I try to be a good guy. And I promise that if you give me a chance, I'll be your good guy."

Before even giving her a chance to respond, Hassan locked their lips together in a passionate kiss, as he wrapped his arms around her and pulled her closer to him on her bed.

Nazariah had no choice but to get lost in the kiss. She didn't want to break away from his lips anyway. It all felt way too good to stop. He knew how to kiss her just right, far better than any other man she had kissed.

When he slowly unlocked their lips, he smirked at her.

"You're so cute," she complimented him with a sweet smile.

"Don't tell nobody I told you that corny shit," he stated seriously. "Especially Khyree."

She nodded, still smiling brightly as she looked up at him.

"And don't be tryin' any funny business tonight, Naz. If I wake up in the middle of the night cause you over here grindin' your ass on a nigga's dick… Just know I'll have to fuck the shit out of that pussy, regardless of how tired you are."

Nazariah's eyes widened with shock at his serious words, before she let out a light giggle.

"I'm not playin', girl."

"Yeah, whatever," she said with a yawn. "Your rude ass really can't do shit."

"Oh word? That's what you believe?"

"That's what I know," she confidently boasted.

"Yeah, we'll see how much talkin' your ass can do once I'm deep in your guts."

Nazariah let out one last giggle before closing her eyes. As rude and cocky as he was, she absolutely loved it.

Hassan gave her one last peck on her lips, then kissed her forehead before shutting his eyes also and going to sleep. The last words he remembered hearing before falling into his deep slumber was, "I've fallen for you, Hassan Knight."

MISS JENESEQUA

$ CHAPTER THIRTEEN $

"What do you mean you're not coming in today, Nazariah? You still need to… What?... Wait, pause. Repeat what you just said… Anthony and Hassan… And Khyree?... You've gotta be kidding me right now… You're with him right now? Damn… Okay, later then… Don't keep me waiting, bitch, you've got a lot of explaining to do. Alright… Talk to you later, girl."

Amina ended her phone call with Nazariah before opening up her locker and chucking her smartphone inside.

It was only 11 a.m. and Amina had already been through so much this morning. So much being Nazariah not coming into work and quickly calling her a few minutes ago to explain what was going on.

She hadn't gone into too much detail but from what Amina had been told so far, Nazariah agreed to go to Anthony's family dinner only to be introduced to his cousin Dominique, who Amina was aware had cancer. Turns out, Dominique was married to Hassan. Which meant that his wife that Nazariah had found out about in the Dominican Republic, was actually Dominique. That meant that Anthony and Hassan were cousins-in-law, including Khyree.

Khyree.

The man that Amina had managed to block out of her thoughts so well. But hearing that Hassan had now popped back up into Nazariah's life had Amina feeling some type of way. Not a bad way about their relationship, shit, she was happy for whatever became of them. As long as Hassan sorted out what he was going to do about Dominique, then she didn't have any issues with him trying to get with her best friend.

A type of way about Khyree.

Ever since they had last spoken in the Dominican Republic, Amina promised herself that she wasn't going to get involved with him. She didn't even need to know him that well enough to know the way he operated. He was a player, and she could see no parts of them being together. Like she had told Nazariah before, she believed he was only talking to her for the sex. And if Amina had given it up to him so quickly, he would have bounced the very first chance he could get.

So quite frankly, she didn't want to get herself involved in all that. Khyree may have been super fine and her type, but she wasn't about to let him get the best of her. She was sticking to her original plan and continuing to pretend that the man didn't exist.

Amina locked her locker before getting up from the silver bench she had been sitting on, and straightening her blue scrubs.

Then, she walked out to head out to see her matron, who she needed to see about the rest of her schedule for the next two weeks.

Amina had been contemplating taking another vacation out of Miami. However, this time she wanted to go alone. Somewhere cold and peaceful, perhaps London. It usually stayed pretty cold there this time of the year; even in the summer, they rarely saw sunny days. She needed another break. She was already sick of Miami.

Amina casually strolled down the white hospital corridors, walking to the matron's office.

"Amina!"

The sudden call of her name had her turning around with curiosity to know who wanted her.

It was Matron.

"Matron," she greeted her warmly. "I was just coming to look for you."

Matron was a 49-year-old woman who was in charge of all the nurses in the Jackson Memorial Hospital. Those nurses included Amina and Nazariah.

She was a mother figure to all the nurses, a wise voice that they could all count on and come to in their times of need. Matron's real

183

name was Claudette. She was a black woman, with brown skin so smooth and wrinkle free that she was the definition of the phrase *'black don't crack.'*

"And I was just coming to look for you," she informed Amina. "There's some guy here at the front, requesting to see you."

"Who?"

"Some guy," Matron stated. "A very fine guy I might add."

Amina was immediately confused. No one ever came to visit her at work. "Did he say what his name was?"

"No, he didn't, but he said he's not going anywhere until you come out and see him."

Who on earth could be so adamant to see her right now? She wasn't expecting to see anybody.

"Alright, I'll go see what he wants. He's at the front reception?"

"Yes, child," Matron responded blissfully. "As soon as you're done seeing to him, come see me and I'll give you your schedule for the upcoming weeks."

"Alright, Matron. Thank you."

Taking one step into the front reception turned out to be

Amina's biggest mistake of the week.

Sitting comfortably on the red waiting seats was the one man that she had convinced herself was never going to enter her life ever again.

Her palms began to feel clammy and her heart quickened, as she watched him stare down at his bright screen, tapping lightly on his screen.

Oh God...

Khyree Knight in the flesh, sitting so handsomely in grey sweats and a fresh white tee. Those muscular arms never looked so good as they did now. On his feet were white Nike sneakers so crisp and clean they looked like they had never touched the floor. *Ever.* He also sported a large gold chain that hung around his neck, two gold studs, and what looked to be an expensive watch, due to the amount of diamonds shining brightly on his wrist.

The wealth of this man was evident and extremely attractive to various nurses eyeing him closely as they walked past, including some waiting female patients who sat near him.

Amina didn't bother trying to figure out why he was here. She just knew that he must have been confused if he believed he was here to see her.

Just as she plucked up the courage to turn around and leave, Khyree's head shot up.

Khyree took one look at her in her nurse's uniform and smiled happily that she was here. She still looked as gorgeous as the time he had seen her lying peacefully on her sun bed. Even in blue nurse scrubs, she was still looking sexy as fuck to him. He loved the fact that he was seeing her in her most natural element right now.

Work.

But seeing her try to leave and run far away from him, had him becoming infuriated.

"Amina, wait!" he shouted, getting up from his seat, seeing her walk away back in the direction she had come from. "I just wanna talk to you!"

Really, he should have been the one running away and getting angry. She was the one that had given him a fake number and refused to actually give him a sincere chance. She had just stringed him along.

"Um, excuse me! Excuse me, young man! You can't go through there," the receptionist barked at him. "Staff only!"

"Man, fuck that!" Khyree yelled before running straight into the hospital zone that Amina had walked straight through. The zone meant only for staff.

He really didn't care. He just wanted her to give him a chance to speak. And he wanted her to tell him exactly why she had given him a fake number.

"Amina!"

Amina stopped in her tracks after realizing that she could still hear Khyree's voice so close and near, despite the fact that she had walked into a staff only zone.

This nigga.

She turned around to face him. "Khyree, what the hell are you doing?" she asked in a tone, half filled with nerves and anger. "You can't be here!"

"I can do whatever the fuck I want," he retorted, walking up to her until he was towering over her. "I need to speak to you, beautiful."

Beautiful. She felt butterflies fly in her stomach hearing him call her that again. The last she had heard that was back in the Dominican Republic. It was what he liked to call her. But Amina figured it was all a part of his game to get her into his bed.

"Well, I don't want to speak to you," she fired back. "How did you even find out where I work? You stalking me now?"

Thanks to Hassan sending him the hospital address of where Nazariah and Amina worked, he was able to be here right now. And he wasn't leaving until he got what he wanted.

"I have my ways," he answered proudly. "Look, shorty, can I just talk to you?"

"You're talking to me right now, aren't you?" Amina smartly questioned.

"In private," he added. "Just you and I."

"No."

"Huh?"

"I said no," Amina replied. "I don't have anything to say to you."

"You don't have anythin' to say to me?"

"No."

"After your rude ass gave me a fake number, you don't have anythin' to say to me?" He queried in a frustrated tone.

Amina kept silent, remembering what she had done.

"I was tryin' to get to know you better and you give me a fake fuckin' number?"

188

She could see how angry he was getting; she could even feel it too. Him towering over her and glaring down at her with all his attention on her, allowed her to tell.

"Like I just said," she began in a voice filled with determination, "I have absolutely nothing to say to you." Just when she turned and began walking away from him, she felt a strong grip pull her back.

She turned around to stare up at him.

"Don't walk away from me, beautiful," he ordered firmly. "I'm being fuckin' serious when I say I need to talk to you."

"And guess what? I'm being just as serious when I say I have nothing to say to you." Amina kept her eyes on his, still nervous, but still feeling brave enough to show him how serious she was in her words.

"Your ass can never quit being so damn stubborn," he commented before letting go of her arm.

"And you'll never stop being so rude!" she shouted.

"Man, shut up with that crap. I came down here to tell you how I feel but because your head is so far up your ass, you don't seem to care about anyone else but how you feel. So fuck you, Amina!"

Amina's feelings were immediately hurt by his cold, harsh

words.

"No, fuck you, Khyree! You're an arrogant, idiotic fool who thinks the whole world revolves around him. Who thinks every single chick wants him. Well, I guess it's time for you to finally wake the fuck up and smell the roses!"

"Don't play yourself, shorty, you know you always wanted me."

"I never wanted you, Khyree, that's what I made you believe. I never liked you, I never wanted you to talk to me, I only tolerated you. Quite frankly, I dislike you. Thinking about you leaves a very bitter taste in my mouth. I don't like you, I hate you."

Ouch.

Khyree's heart felt like it had suddenly been pierced with tiny pins coming in at all different types of directions. That's how much her words had cut deep.

He knew it. He had even told Hassan that she was never really feeling him like that. And now he had made himself look like a damn fool, coming over to her work and demanding to see her.

She hates me.

Khyree simply nodded at her before taking a few steps away from her.

"Khyree, I—"

"I apologize for bothering you, shorty," he sincerely stated, interrupting her words. "It won't happen again."

Then he turned on his heels and began walking back to the front reception.

Leaving a guilty Amina, who was hating herself for creating such silly lies. Silly lies that had hurt him.

She didn't hate him. She didn't hate him one bit.

***

Nazariah bit her lips sexily, feeling her pussy heat up with excitement at the fact that he had nothing but a white towel wrapped around his waist.

She couldn't help but eye fuck his wet body, admiring every single muscle on his body that had been shaped to heavenly perfection by the very gods themselves.

Those tatted arms that had been wrapped around her body all night were only reminding her of how good it felt to be in his arms. And how badly she wanted to be in them again.

Damn, why was he so fine?

"I see your ass wants to start somethin' again, Naz," Hassan spoke up, grinning as he watched her watching him. She shyly looked away until she no longer felt his gaze on her. Then she continued to eye fuck him again.

They had yet to have sex and it was killing Nazariah. She didn't even understand how she had peacefully slept in his arms, even after feeling his big friend poke her behind all night. How had she managed to do it?

She didn't know why they hadn't had sex yet, but Hassan wasn't pressing it and neither was she. Whenever it happened, it happened. But Nazariah wouldn't mind it happening now.

Hassan grabbed the bottle of coconut lotion from Nazariah's pink dresser before making his way to the edge of her bed and sitting down.

Nazariah lay still on her bed, still keeping both eyes on him. Since his back was facing her, that's the main thing her eyes were focused on. And the more she stared at it, the more she imagined herself clawing away at his back as he fucked he—

"Miss Shyness," he called out to her. "Come rub my back." Hearing him call her the nickname he had first given her when they had met that day on the beach, had her glowing with joy. He was the only person who could call her that and have her feeling so happy.

"Where's your manners?" she asked, pulling her covers off her body and moving across her bed to where he was.

The touch of her soft hands on his shoulders made Hassan's dick turn hard. It was the way that she knew how to touch him so effortlessly to make him feel good that had him blown away. She was his calm and pleasure all in one.

"You already know how much of a gentleman I am, girl. Who made you breakfast in bed this morning?" he asked her curiously.

"Mmm, you did."

"Exactly," he happily sang, shutting his eyes as her soft hands began to rub on his back. "Feels good, baby..."

Nazariah had decided to not go into work today due to Hassan wanting to spend some quality time with her. She wasn't usually one to miss work often so she figured one day couldn't hurt. So she called in sick. Besides, after Hassan admitting his feelings to her, she wanted to spend some time with him. Especially since she knew she felt the same way about him.

The only thing on her mind right now was figuring out a way to break things off with Anthony.

If she was going to give Hassan a chance, then Anthony needed to go. It might have seemed cruel that she was willing to ditch their relationship so quick, but she would rather be cruel than string Anthony along. Her feelings for Hassan were stronger and deeper. And that's just the way shit was.

Once she was done applying lotion to his back, Nazariah leaned close to the side of his neck before gently planting soft kisses on his skin.

Fresh out the shower and she absolutely loved everything about the way he smelled right now. He had used her bath soap and it had him smelling like roses, but Nazariah didn't mind at all. He smelt wonderful to her.

It didn't take long for her neck kisses to turn heated even further, and before Hassan could realize it, Nazariah had whipped off his white towel, leaving him completely naked on her bed.

"Fuuuck," he passionately groaned.

While one hand dug into his thigh, her other hand was wrapped tightly around his dick, smoothly moving up and down it.

Nazariah hadn't had her mouth on him since they had been in Dominican Republic together, and having him now brought back freaky memories. Freaky memories that she couldn't wait to relive and recreate. And also, make new ones.

"Naz... Shit, girl."

The second her full lips wrapped around his mushroom head, Hassan could already feel himself quickly getting closer to the edge.

She had already been driving him wild with all the stroking she had been doing. But now that she had her mouth on him, things were about to get even nastier.

Her head began to bob up and down between his legs as she sucked his hard shaft vigorously and with great momentum. Her tongue constantly swirled around his long length, creating a sort of roller coaster effect on his dick.

"N-Nazar... Nazariah, goddamn you makin' a nigga lose his mind right now. Agh!"

She couldn't help but smile to herself. She had definitely missed being able to make him feel this good.

Up. Down. She sucked, she licked, she stroked, even kissed and got sloppy for him.

Hassan's eyes widened with pure lust as he watched Nazariah spit on his dick, then clear up all the nasty mess she had created.

"You nasty girl," he whispered with delight, running his fingers through her hair and beginning to guide her head up and down his rod. Fucking her mouth at the speed that he desired. He

195

went as slow or as fast as he fancied, loving the view of Nazariah's mouth filled with nothing but his dick.

He had a feeling she hardly gave head to her nigga and if she did, she ain't ever do it like this. He had turned her into his personal freak. She was like this for nobody else but him.

Ten minutes later, Hassan had her completely naked for him and his body on top of hers. His lips moved to the side of her neck only to hover above her ear, so he could whisper seductively to her. "You the only woman I've ever wanted to make love to this bad."

Nazariah's eyes shut as she listened to his sweet whispers and felt his soft lips kiss on her skin.

"Ugh... Hassan!" Nazariah cried as Hassan's thickness suddenly invaded her wet cave.

Finally, she was getting to have him in the way she loved the most.

***

"Slow the fuck down nigga and start again. Who did what?"

Nazariah's eyes fluttered open only for her to remember where she still was. On the top of her bed, completely naked and very sore.

She wasn't sure what time it was, but she knew it had to be deep into the afternoon. With the amount of sex she had been having today, she felt like she needed a damn cigarette.

Hassan wasn't on the bed next to her and she couldn't see him in her bedroom, but she could definitely hear him.

"I swear I'ma kill these niggas myself with the way they keep losin' my shit," he raged. "All those niggas gon' be buried six feet in the ground. Nah, I'm not playin'. This is the second mothafuckin' time. Do they not know who the fuck I am?"

Nazariah's ears were at full alert now that she could hear Hassan on the phone. She had no clue with who though. By the sounds of things, he wasn't happy and he wanted people dead. What the hell?

She was aware that Hassan was crazy, but not the type of crazy to want to kill people.

"I'll be home later on today. Find that nigga and have him at the main trap tonight. Since he likes to freely let the next fool steal my shit for free, I got somethin' for his dumb ass. Dealing with him once and for all tonight! I ain't taking this disrespect no more. Maybe when he stops breathing, he'll learn his lesson."

Nazariah's heart almost stopped at Hassan's violent words. She felt her whole body freezing with fright. His words echoed in her head.

"When he stops breathing, he'll learn his lesson."

Damn.

Who the hell was this crazy, attractive man she had fallen for?

$ CHAPTER FOURTEEN $

"You go first."

"No you."

"Bitch, you have the most to say."

"But you have shit to say too. Go first, Mina. Please," Nazariah pleaded with puppy dog eyes. "Pleaseeeeee."

Amina quickly waved her off before grabbing her a glass of wine, gently taking a sip and then breathing softly.

"Khyree came to see me at work," Amina announced.

"What?" Nazariah's eyes widened with complete surprise. "How'd he find out where you work?"

"The same way Hassan found out where you lived," she suggested. "These niggas been stalking us."

Nazariah lightly chuckled before reaching for her wine glass setting on the coffee table in front of them both.

"He said he wanted to talk to me. I told him to fuck off. Boohoo, the end."

"Amina, no! You didn't."

"I did," she proudly said before deciding to come clean about what had really happened, seeing Nazariah eye her suspiciously. "I didn't want to talk to him, Nazariah, and he kept pushing the conversation. We started going at it, you know how we get, and I ended up hurting his feelings... He stormed off."

"Damn, what exactly did you say?" Nazariah queried, her voice full of wonder.

"Told him that I never wanted him, that's what I made him believe. I never liked him, I never wanted him to talk to me, I only tolerated him... I dislike him. Also told him how thinking about him leaves a very bitter taste in my mouth," she informed Nazariah quietly, still feeling guilty about the whole entire situation.

"Shit," Nazariah cursed. "That's cold, girl."

"Told him I hate him, too," Amina whispered, shutting her eyes in embarrassment.

"Mina!"

"I tried to say sorry! But the fool wouldn't hear me out, would he?"

"Mina, I knew you were rude but... Shit, girl," Nazariah commented before chuckling. "I don't get why you're so mean towards him when you know how much you like him."

"I don't like him," Amina mumbled.

Nazariah shot her a frown.

"Okay, maybe I do... But I don't think that us being together is a good idea."

"And why exactly do you think that?"

"He's a player."

"Hassan was a player... He's even married, but he wants me and I want him too. So I'm giving him a chance, I guess," Nazariah explained. "I think you should give Khyree a chance too."

"Speaking of Hassan," Amina began happily, "tell me everything."

Nazariah took another sip of her wine, a few sips, before telling Amina the whole situation from the very beginning. To how she had met Hassan at Anthony's family dinner, finding out they were cousins, unable to think straight with him being right in front of her. Then explaining how he came over to her apartment, attempted to pick her lock because she refused to let him in at first, and then her letting him in. Them talking, going at it for a bit before Nazariah finally gave in.

"So you slept butt ass naked in his arms?" Amina questioned with a smirk. "Without you or him trying anything?"

Nazariah nodded before replying, "We had sex the next

morning though."

"Of course you did," Amina knowingly responded. "With the way you've been moving like lovers madly in love, how could you not?"

"We're not lovers, Mina, we're just…. Testing the waters."

"Testing the whole damn ocean more like," Amina laughed. "What about his wife? What about Anthony? Have you figured out how you're going to handle all of that?"

"I know I'm breaking up with Anthony," Nazariah voiced. "I'm just not sure when."

"Well, hurry up and make it soon, bitch," Amina warned. "You don't want him anymore, so you need to cut him loose before you get into something you can't handle."

"I will… I will."

"And Dominique? What did Hassan say about her?"

Nazariah kept quiet and looked down at her hands, not really sure what to tell Amina. Hassan hadn't said anything about Dominique. Other than she was sick and he wasn't going to leave her hanging, in her last few months of life.

Nazariah instantly felt her chin being lifted up and she was back into staring into Amina's pretty brown eyes.

"Zariah," she sternly called her.

"He hasn't said anything."

Amina let go off her chin before shaking her head with disapproval. "Then you better leave him alone."

"She's sick, Mina! He's just trying to be there for her until she dies."

"How long has she got?"

"Just a couple more months."

"Alright then, can she hurry up and die already?"

"Mina!" Nazariah covered her mouth to stop the laughter that was trying to escape her lips. "You're going to hell. Definitely, going to hell."

"What?" Amina laughed loudly. "Like, she's wasting people's time."

"Stop, Mina," Nazariah chuckled lightly. "Stop it."

"Alright, alright. So when are you next seeing him?"

"He wants to see me tonight. He's got a club re-opening tonight but I'm not sure I'm going."

"Why not?"

"I overheard him say some shit to someone on the phone and it's got me kinda scared," Nazariah admitted.

"What kinda shit?" Amina curiously asked.

"Talking about how he's gonna kill some niggas and something about when someone's stopped breathing they'll finally learn their lesson."

"Damn."

"I know… I mean, I like him and all, but now that I think about it, I don't really know him that well. We spent a lot of time in the Dominican getting to know each other, but not well enough. I mean, I told him everything about me, he told me some shit about him, but it wasn't a lot. Clearly not enough for me to find out he has a wife until the very end."

"So you feel like he's hiding some more stuff from you?"

Nazariah shook her head 'yes' before sighing. "And I have a feeling it's some shit that I'm not gonna like."

***

"Hassan, you hardly sleep in the house anymore, I don't understand what I've done wrong to you."

Hassan continued to fix his black Burberry tuxedo in the large mirror in front of him, trying his hardest to block Dominique out. She just didn't know when to quit.

"Hassan, I'm talking to you, nigga!"

"And you need to shut the fuck up with all that talking in my ear," he snapped, turning around to face her, sitting on the edge of the beige California king sized bed. The bed he never slept in. If he was spending the night in his mansion, he was sleeping in one of his guest rooms.

"Hassan, I love you."

Hassan slowly turned back around to face the mirror in front of him. He wished he could say the same to her, but he couldn't. Not when he was falling in love with somebody completely different.

"Hassan, don't you love me?"

Nah, Dominique, I really don't. But he couldn't dare bring himself to tell her that. He knew how bad it would hurt her, so he continued to stay silent and fix his bowtie.

"Hassan!"

"Chill," he warned her in a furious tone. "Look, I ain't got time for this tonight, Dominique. I've got somewhere to be. Get some rest, take your meds, and call your nurse to bring you up whatever

206

you need."

"What if I need you?"

"You only call in emergencies, Dominique, nothing else."

"But what if I just need you as my husband, to be by my side?" she questioned desperately, but Hassan was no longer listening. He was too busy tapping away on his phone to the only girl he wanted to be with right now.

She was pissing him off right now though.

What do you mean you ain't coming, Naz? he typed back.

Nazariah: *Exactly what I just said Hassan. I'm not coming tonight.*

Hassan: *Yes you are. Quit playing with a nigga.*

Nazariah: *I don't feel like coming out tonight.*

Hassan: *So you don't want to see me?*

Nazariah: *I never said that.*

Hassan: *Well the way you acting tells me that.*

Nazariah: *I just don't want to come out. I have work tomorrow.*

Hassan: *You already agreed to come when I first told you. This* *ain't up for fucking discussion girl, you coming. I'll send the car over for you in an hour.*

Nazariah: *I'm not coming Hassan! Just let it go.*

Nazariah clearly must have lost her mind if she believed that Hassan was letting this go. He wasn't letting this go at all. So he decided to call her, only to be further pissed that she was taking so long to pick up her phone.

"Yo, what the fuck is wrong with you? You told me the first time you were coming so you're coming. I'm not in the mood for this tonight," he snapped, walking out the bedroom and getting ready to leave his crib. His driver was already parked outside and ready for him to head to his club.

Tonight he was re-opening after deciding to close the club three months ago for a complete makeover of its appearance, not to mention he had also decided to hire new people.

"Hassan, I'm not," she sternly voiced.

"Be ready in an hour, Nazariah, or I swear to God I'ma come down to that apartment and drag your dumb ass out myself," he concluded before hanging up the phone on her.

He was already not in the mood because of Dominique annoying him tonight, but for Nazariah to now be trying him? He was surely about to lose it if he didn't calm himself down.

Nazariah was coming tonight and that was that.

An hour later and Hassan had arrived at his *Legacy* night club, showed face, and thanked everyone for coming tonight. His mood had completely changed for the better now that he was here, and seeing all the preparation for his night club finally come to life.

Hassan looked to his left to see Khyree chatting up some girl he had let into VIP and decided to rock with for the night. He then looked to his right only for a large grin to form on his face once he locked eyes with the beautiful goddess he couldn't get enough of.

"Miss Shyness, you supposed to be smiling. Why ain't you smiling, baby?"

Nazariah rolled her eyes at him before looking away and turning to face Amina. Amina, who couldn't keep her eyes off Khyree and the random he had brought into the VIP section they were designated in. Nazariah could see how jealous she was; it was written all over her face.

"Amina, you okay, hun?" Nazariah asked her girl, feeling Hassan sit directly next to her with his body touching hers.

She was still so angry with him for forcing her to come to his club tonight. She had work tomorrow and she wasn't in the mood for all this. But she couldn't lie, seeing how successful his club was doing had her pleased for Hassan. He was really doing well for himself. The amount of people packed up in here tonight was unreal. And the amount of eyes on her right now wasn't something she was used to. All these females eyeing her with envy wasn't something she had ever experienced before. This was all new to her.

"I'm fine," Amina said loudly over the upbeat music. "You?"

"Baby."

Nazariah ignored Hassan calling her and continued to converse with Amina. "I'm okay, just not really wanting to be here right now but some rich fool made me come."

"Amina, tell your friend I said she needs to lose the fuckin' attitude," Hassan informed Amina smoothly. "She's supposed to have a good time with me tonight."

Amina lightly giggled before grabbing her champagne glass.

"Amina, tell the rich fool I said he needs to stop thinking he's the boss of me. I don't want to have a good time with him tonight."

Hassan leaned in closer to Nazariah's ear so that he could privately whisper to her. "I really want you have to have a good time with me tonight, Miss Shyness."

210

"Well I really don't want to have…"

The sudden lick of her earlobe had her words trailing off, a shiver running up her spine, and a pool forming in her panties.

"I can't wait to have you tonight," he continued to whisper sexily in her ear, his deep, husky voice turning her on even more. "All of you… Out of that sexy ass dress… Completely naked for me…"

Nazariah's breathing suddenly caught in her throat as she listened to him, seducing her with just his words alone.

She turned her head so that she could stare into those enchanting green eyes of his and get lost into them, just like she always did.

The second he gently branded his lips down to hers, Nazariah knew she was no longer angry with him. All types of negative feelings that she had been feeling had now disappeared. And for the rest of the night, she was going to enjoy being in his company.

She loved the way he was dressed tonight. In an expensive custom tailored tux, matching black bowtie, and smart black lace ups on his feet. This was the first time she was seeing him in a suit, and she was absolutely loving it. He looked so damn sexy to her right now.

"Did I tell you how handsome you look tonight?" she asked him shyly, watching as he poured them both some more champagne from the bottle he had picked up out their ice bucket.

"Did I tell you how sexy you look in that dress?"

She gave him a cheerful smile before running her fingers through his soft curls and letting him give her a sip from his glass.

While they kissed, drank and talked to one another, Amina couldn't keep her eyes off this thirty ass chick all up on Khyree.

She was touching him any chance she got, constantly giggling and flirting with him. It was driving Amina crazy and she was starting to regret agreeing to come here with Nazariah in the very first place.

"Is there a problem?"

Amina's eyebrows furrowed in anger and her eyes squinted with confusion.

"Excuse me?"

"You heard me," the thirsty groupie all up on Khyree said. "Is there a problem? 'Cause you can't seem to take your eyes off me and Khy."

Amina was honestly confused. Who the hell was this chick

talking to?

"It's a free country. I look wherever the hell I want to look, girl," Amina commented.

"Clearly, you see something you want but can't have, with the way you keep constantly staring over here," the girl retorted.

"Oh no, I see something I definitely *don't* want," Amina said with a fake smile, staring at Khyree in particular.

"What the hell is that supposed to mean?"

Nazariah could smell the drama already and she was ready to back her girl any time some shit popped off.

"I don't want a guy that's had some ratchet ass chick touching all up on him. Seems like the person with the problem here is you, 'cause you can't seem to take your damn hands off him and his dick."

"Bitch, you mad cause you can't have his fine ass? You want him that bad?" the girl boasted with a smirk. "He's mine tonight."

Khyree was about to intervene and say that he wasn't anyone's tonight, but he didn't want to intervene just yet. He was loving how Amina was coming quick with the insults and quite frankly, it was turning him on to see that smart mouth of hers in action again.

213

"Uh-uh, definitely not mad. Unlike you, I'm not thirsty for some dick tonight," Amina stated casually.

"Thirsty? You're the one looking over here! You need to go seek some help. Maybe someone can help you with your inability to not accept what you can't have," the groupie spat.

"You know what you need? Some damn water. Walmart has their great value water, 24 for $5. Get some for your thirsty ass, little girl."

Nazariah, Hassan and Khyree couldn't help but smirk at Amina's words.

"I swear I'ma smack somebody in this fucking room," the groupie yelled.

Amina suddenly looked around, turning in her seat trying to figure out which room she was talking about, 'cause it certainly couldn't have been this one. "Which room? Better be some other room 'cause if it's this room you're about to get your ass whooped."

"Stupid as—"

Nazariah interrupted her. "I suggest you keep your mouth shut or you'll be leaving here tonight in the back of an ambulance."

"What did you just say?"

214

"Are you deaf?" Nazariah challenged her. "You heard what the hell I just said."

"A'ight, that's enough," Hassan intervened, seeing that Nazariah was getting involved in the rising tension. "Lady, leave."

The groupie gave him a frown. "Me?"

"No, the bitch sitting next to you," he fired back in an annoyed tone. "You. Get the fuck out."

"Khyree, tell hi—"

"I think it's best you go," Khyree told her gently. "I'll catch up with you later."

The groupie got up and stormed out the VIP section, leaving Khyree, Amina, Nazariah and Hassan.

Khyree took one look at Amina only to be surprised by what he was seeing. Amina was now eating the ice cubes out of the champagne bucket.

"Yo, what the hell are you doing?" he asked her, full of confusion.

Nazariah answered for her though. "It's a way of cooling herself down. Keeping herself calm, you know, especially when she's pissed."

"So she eats ice?" Khyree continued to ask.

"Yup."

"She's fuckin' crazy, yo," Khyree commented.

"No… I ain't," Amina responded, munching on her piece of ice.

"Yes you are," he repeated with a smirk. "Fuckin' crazy."

"Shut up."

"Make me," Khyree voiced boldly. "But your crazy ass wouldn't dare."

"Is that so?"

"Absolutely."

Amina decided to keep quiet and just continue to eat her ice before she ended up saying something she regretted. She was sick of Khyree and the way he made her feel.

"I just can't get why she won't admit that she wants me, Nazariah," Khyree told Nazariah. "She wants me!"

Khyree was sure of it now. Even though she had claimed that she didn't, that had all been a lie. Seeing how jealous she was when he was with some chick proved that to him. She was feeling

216

him all along and just fronting like she wasn't.

"No I don't."

"Yes you do," he pushed. "You've wanted me from the jump but you won't admit it!"

"Nigga, in your dreams. In your motherfucking dreams."

"In my dreams, we were fucking and you kept telling me on and on how much you loved this dick."

Nazariah couldn't help but gasp and Amina only felt herself being riled up with more frustration.

"Nigga, fuck you!"

Khyree sat up straight in his seat, staring straight at Amina with conviction. "Fuck you, Amina!"

"And who are *you* yelling at?"

"You!"

"Your dick ain't big enough to catch an attitude with me. You better lower your voice," she ordered.

"So you've seen my dick?"

"No, but I—"

"Unless you've seen it, had it balls deep in you, in your mouth,

217

don't speak on it," he snapped at her.

Amina decided to stop talking to him and keep any more words she had to say, to herself. Fuck Khyree Knight and his cocky, fine ass.

"Hassan, thanks for inviting me and Naz tonight, but I'm gonna catch a cab home now," Amina announced coolly.

"A cab?" Nazariah asked. "I guess I better get going too."

"Baby, I still want you here with me," Hassan requested lovingly.

"No, hun, you don't need to follow me. I'll catch an Uber, I'll be fine."

"I'll drop you home," Khyree announced cheerfully.

"Like I just said, Nazariah, I'm cool with catching an Uber. I don't need no idiot taking me home," Amina said, in directing to Khyree.

"Like I just said, I'll drop you home."

But Amina had already given Nazariah a kiss goodnight and was fast on her heels out the VIP section.

"Hassan, you were right," Khyree voiced as he stood up the plush sofa. "I do like her. As annoying and crazy as she is, I really like her."

"You sure, bro?"

"Positive," Khyree concluded before chasing after Amina, determined to give her a ride home.

Leaving Hassan and Nazariah in the VIP section alone. Hassan wrapped his arm tighter around her waist, pulling her closer towards him before beginning to kiss on her neck.

"I guess it's just you and me," she whispered.

"Uh-huh…" He continued to kiss on her neck, making her feel good.

Just when Nazariah could feel his hands moving up her dress, he suddenly stopped due to someone calling for him.

"Boss. You're needed downstairs."

Hassan turned to face Ice, his right-hand man, with a frown. "Why?"

"He's here."

Hassan quickly nodded before turning back round to face Nazariah.

"I'm sorry I need to leave right now, Naz, but I'll be back in a bit, baby. Don't go anywhere."

"I won't," she assured him before cupping the side of his face once he pecked her lips. He couldn't just leave her with one, so he pecked her a few more times before their mouths stayed locked for a few more seconds, passionately meshing together.

"I gotta go," he reminded her, pulling their lips apart and sighing deeply. "Don't leave, Miss Shyness."

And then just like that, he was gone, leaving Nazariah all by herself in the club, bobbing her head to the music being played by the DJ, and drinking her glass of champagne.

It was only 15 minutes later when Nazariah was suddenly joined by someone. She couldn't make out who it was until they entered the VIP section and came closer to her.

"Dominique?"

Dominique took a good look at the stunning woman sitting down in front of her before quickly taking a seat next to her.

"Nazariah? What are you doing here?"

Nazariah couldn't even hide her shock well enough. Dominique was here. In the flesh. Fully dressed for the club and everything.

Why would Hassan embarrass her like this?

"Khyree invited my friend and I, to Hassan's club tonight," she lied. "I think he has a crush on my girl." That bit wasn't a lie. It was evident with the way Khyree and Amina were constantly at each other's throats that they liked each other.

"Oh, I see," Dominique answered with a small smile. "I'm glad to see you. I can't seem to find Hassan anywhere, have you seen him?"

Nazariah shook her head 'no'.

"I need to tell him the good news I found out about my cancer."

Nazariah was fully alert now. She found it slightly odd that at 11:30 p.m. was the time that Dominique had chosen to discuss her cancer though.

"I've found out that my treatment is working so well, that I'm going to live much longer than expected. Well, that's what my doctor says anyways."

"Oh wow." Disappointment filled Nazariah. "That's amazing, Dominique. Congratulations. Would you excuse me for a minute? I just need to use the restroom."

"No problem. If you see Hassan on your way over there, don't tell him I'm here. I want it to be a surprise."

No fucking problem, wifey, Nazariah mused to herself, her displeasure building.

Instead of going to the restroom, Nazariah decided to head into the direction that she had seen Hassan walk in. She was completely done with this whole club night of his, but before she left, she wanted to make sure that he got a piece of her mind.

***

"Please, Boss! Boss, pl—"

"Stop all the damn cryin'," Hassan barked, sending another jab onto Kingsley's jaw. "I'm still gonna fuck you up, Kingsley, for losing my shit once again!"

"It was'n—"

Pow! Pow! Pow!

All Hassan could see was red. He no longer cared about what Kingsley had to say. He had heard enough of the bullshit. His only agenda tonight was beating this nigga to the pulp.

Pow! Pow! Pow!

"Boss," Kingsley cried out in agony, his whole entire face now covered with blood. His eye was now black, his lip busted, and his

222

nose gushing out blood. He was coughing up blood too. "Just he—
"

"Aww man… You made me get your blood on my favorite shirt," Hassan announced with a pout, pointing down to his shirt where Kingsley's blood stains were splattered. "My favorite mothafuckin' shirt."

"Boss, just hear me ou—"

"Nah," Hassan cut him off, lifting up Kingsley's chin so he was forced to stare up into his green eyes. "I'm done with listenin' to your bitch ass. I warned you *not* to fuck up again."

"I di—"

Pow! Pow! Pow!

Kingsley continued to throw hard punches onto Kingsley's face, continuing to batter him some more. This nigga had already crossed him once; he couldn't allow it to happen a third time.

Pow! Pow!

"Boss."

Pow! Pow! Pow!

"Boss."

Hassan stopped beating up Kingsley, who was about to pass out from all the punches, and exhaled deeply. He was now wondering why the hell he was being called by one of his boys standing behind him. "What?"

"Female in the room."

Hassan's heart almost stopped after hearing that.

He turned around to the door, only to see his beautiful, teary eyed Miss Shyness, watching him with so much fear and hate.

"Nazariah," he shakily whispered. "Naz, baby I…"

She didn't bother waiting around hearing the bullshit explanation he had to explain about the shit she had just witnessed. She quickly left the room, trying to get as far as possible as she could from him.

"WHY THE FUCK DID YOU NIGGAS LEAVE THE DOOR UNLOCKED?!" Hassan roared, rolling down his bloody sleeves and grabbing his blazer jacket from one of his men.

He ran out, placing his jacket over his body and buttoning up, trying to conceal Kingsley's blood stains that were all over his white shirt. He had no time to change into a new one, he just needed to get to her.

But that was easier said than done once entering the main club area and unable to find her through the crowded room.

Where the fuck had she gone to?

Just when things couldn't get any worse, Hassan's eyes wondered to the VIP area only to see Dominique sitting peacefully, sipping on some alcohol and moving her head to the music.

Fuck his life right now.

MISS JENESEQUA

$ CHAPTER FIFTEEN $

"Nazariah, pick up the damn phone, I just wanna explain."

She wasn't picking up.

"Naz... Please, just let me fuckin' explain."

Not one single call.

"So this is really what your stubborn ass gon' do? Just keep sendin' me straight to voicemail. A'ight, I see how the fuck it is."

She wasn't even giving him a chance to explain anything.

"Keep ignoring a nigga and the next time I see your ass, you in some serious trouble."

And that's what really angered him the most.

***

"You stole our shit twice, and now you wanna come work for us. This is just hella funny," Khyree commented with a hand running across his smooth chin. "Bro, ain't this shit funny?"

Hassan simply nodded, choosing to remain silent, but keeping both eyes plastered on the man in front of him.

Mario Garcia.

The leader of the Leones, the squad that was repeatedly

stealing stock from the Jamaicans, only pissing off The Knight Brothers.

They had done it twice and gotten away with it. Hassan and Khyree were adamant to make sure that there wasn't going to be a third time. However, Mario showing up on their doorstep now had them very suspicious and slightly confused.

What was he up to?

"I apologize for the thefts," Mario Garcia spoke up. "It won't happen again."

Hassan continued to stare straight at him, observing the way his hazel eyes constantly shifted around the room, like he was waiting for the unexpected. Hassan examined everything about the stranger sitting in front of him. From his pale olive skin, his dry pink lips, to those sharp brown eyes. But examining him wasn't doing much in giving Hassan an idea as for why this man was here?

What exactly did he want?

"What do you want?" Hassan queried humbly.

"Like I said before, I want to work for The Knight Brothers," he announced. "I've heard nothing but good shit about you guys and I know that my squad stealing from your boys wasn't a good

228

start, but I didn't even know they worked for you."

Bullshit, Hassan mused. There wasn't a damn person residing in Miami that was part of the drug trade, that didn't know about the Jamaicans working for The Knight Brothers.

"Why steal from them in the first place? Why not just come straight to us?"

"I needed stock and I wasn't sure you guys would give it to me. Especially with me and my squad being new on the scene."

He had a point. The Knight Brothers most certainly didn't just work with any Tom, Dick or Harry. They had to know they could trust who they worked with and could deal with them without any major problems.

"You've caused a lot of issues between us and the Jamaicans," Khyree announced sternly. "Why the hell would we want to work with you, now?"

"Because I've got a hardworking squad filled with guys ready to work and make you guys a whole lot of fucking money."

"Is that so?" Khyree asked with a raised brow, clearly not impressed. "We already have guys who make us a whole lot of fucking money. Who says we need more of you?"

"I think it'll be a good idea for you to let us come work with you," Mario explained simply. "Then you won't have no more problems with your Jamaicans."

"Is that a threat?" Hassan spoke up, sensing some type of threatening manner in his words.

"No," Mario said lightly with a small smile. "Just some honest advice."

"Well stop with the advice," Hassan berated. "No one fuckin' asked."

Mario kept silent.

"As for you wanting to work with my brother and I, we're goin' to think about it."

"We are?" Khyree questioned with confusion.

"We are. And we'll let you know our decision. Entender?" *(Understand?)*

Mario slowly nodded before responding, "Si, jefe." *(Yes, boss.)*

Hassan had to make sure he could trust Mario, and right now he just wasn't sure. He knew that Khyree didn't want any parts of the Leones selling their drugs, but Hassan didn't want to turn down the offer straight away. He needed to have a real long talk with Blaze to find out why he had kicked the Leones out of Atlanta in the first place.

What the hell had he done wrong?

***

"So that's it, you're never going to see him ever again?"

Nazariah shrugged her shoulders not really knowing what to say. She took another bite of her ham sandwich and hungrily chewed away.

"You didn't even give him a chance to explain though."

Nazariah swallowed her food before replying, "Amina, he doesn't deserve an explanation. I know what he does. He kills people who gets on the wrong side of him. He was going to kill that man if I didn't walk in."

"But you don't know exactly why he wa—"

"And I really don't want to find out. Amina, please stop defending him. It's over."

"Bu—"

"Amina," Nazariah cut her off, shooting her a rude stare. "It's over. Let it go."

"Alright, alright." Amina threw her hands up in surrender

before lifting her peanut butter sandwich to her lips. "I'll let it go."

The two ladies began to eat their lunch in silence, staring around at their peaceful surroundings. They were currently having their lunch break outside the hospital canteen. There were tables and seats enabling the nurses and doctors to come outside into the warm weather to eat instead of staying cooped up inside.

So Amina and Nazariah decided to have their lunch outside today, wanting to enjoy the peaceful warm Miami air.

However, things weren't peaceful for long. Because as soon as Nazariah took one last bite of her sandwich, a loud booming sound of music filled her eardrums.

These bitches be nagging the kid

Fuck it, it is what it is, if you get hit you get hit

I don't forget or forgive

Drake & Future's "Digital Dash" only seemed to get louder and louder and it wasn't until Nazariah's head shot up from her food that she noticed the red Lamborghini pull up in the staff parking lot, right in front of where she and Amina sat.

She stared at it with annoyance, hearing the music go down, as the tinted car window suddenly rolled down. Once his handsome face appeared and those gorgeous eyes locked onto her, her anger

232

mounted.

Why was he here?!

"Yo! Nazariah!" he shouted at her from his car. "Get in."

He must have lost his damn mind if he believed that she was obeying anything he had to say. What he really needed to do was leave.

"Nazariah, you hear me talkin' to you!"

Nazariah continued to ignore him, looking away and trying to focus her concentration on something else. She pulled out her phone, hoping it would be a good distraction.

"Naz!"

It wasn't.

"Get your ass in this mothafuckin' car before I come over there and knock your stupid ass out," he raged. "I ain't fuckin' playin' with you, girl."

"Zariah, maybe you should just go," Amina whispered to her. "It's obvious he wants to see you."

"And I really don't give a—"

"NAZARIAH!"

Nazariah's head shot back up so she was now looking into his green eyes.

"Get in this fuckin' car, right now."

From the crazy look in his eyes, she knew that if she didn't listen she was going to be in for some trouble.

***

They sat in silence. He looked at her while she looked out the window, wanting to be somewhere else. Far, far away from here.

When he tried to reach for her hand across from his seat, she moved her hand away, not wanting to feel his touch. His touch that only made her weak.

"Nazariah, please just hear me out," he begged, reaching for her hand once more. Seeing that she hadn't moved it away, he continued speaking. "I apologize for what you saw. I never ever wanted you to see that side of me."

"What side of you?" she queried innocently, turning around to face him. "The violent side of you that kills people who get on the wrong side of you?"

"Yes," he seriously replied. "And I'll kill you if you ever try to leave me."

"You better be joking," she said, not afraid of his words. He liked to threaten her all the time and by now she was used to it. But seeing him almost beat some guy to death? That was on another level altogether.

"I ain't," he voiced. "But like I was saying before, I never wanted you to see that side of me. And now that you have, I'm gonna explain if you let me."

"Alright, go ahead then. Explain."

"Remember when I told you in the Dominican that I own a few businesses?"

Nazariah simply nodded.

"Well one of those businesses involves me being a distributor."

"A distributor? Of what?" she curiously asked.

"Drugs."

Within the next hour, Nazariah was told everything. Hassan didn't know why he felt like he could trust her but he just felt like he could. So he let her know as much as he could, explaining why she had seen him do what he had done that night.

All Nazariah could do was listen carefully to everything Hassan revealed to her. She knew that the man she had been

MISS JENESEQUA

messing with was dangerous, but not fully aware of just how dangerous. Now she was aware. He was sexy, crazy and extremely dangerous. And she was falling deeply for him, more and more.

The more he told her, the more she should have been wanting to run away, but she wasn't. She only found herself wanting to run closer to him. Run so close that she could be with him alone. And she figured that's exactly what she was going to do.

"You scared?"

Nazariah looked up at Hassan, feeling his strong arms tighten around her body.

They were back at her apartment, cuddling in bed. After Hassan revealed everything to her, he took her to get some lunch and then they headed back to hers.

"No," she whispered before softly pecking his lips. "Should I be?"

"Yeah, you should be," he stated. "But I've got you. So ain't nothin' gon' happen to you because you're mine, Naz. You got that? You're mine."

"I'm yours," she said in agreement, smiling as he kissed her forehead.

She didn't want to kill their loving mood at this moment in

time, but there was something that she really had to get off her chest.

"Dominique spoke to me, that night at your club."

Hassan's eyes widened with worry. "What did she say to you?"

"That her cancer treatment is working better than expected," announced Nazariah. "She'll live much longer than originally thought."

"And what did you say?"

"I said 'congratulations'," Nazariah told him. "I'm happy for her. I'm not sure where this leaves us though, and I know I just said I'm yours, but if she's still gonna be in the picture then I—"

"She's in stage four cancer, Naz," Hassan interrupted her. "The cancer has spread and is still spreading to different major areas of her body daily, any treatment she's getting is only helping her get through it. I've had conversations with her doctors, they're only trying to keep her hopes up. The life expectancy for pancreatic cancer isn't high at all. She's still going to die in the next few months. No one can stop that."

"Oh."

Nazariah didn't know what else to say. Dominique seemed so happy and grateful that she had more time to live. But now it

237

seemed like she didn't.

"I want to be with you, Nazariah," Hassan voiced lovingly. "Only you."

"I want to be with you too," she replied before resting her head back onto his hard chest.

The only thing she needed to do now, was figure out how she was breaking up with Anthony.

$ CHAPTER SIXTEEN $

"I say we work with them."

"Work with them? You sure, bro?"

"Yeah," Hassan stated coolly into the phone. "But warn them and make sure they know not to fuck with us. Or shit ain't gon' be pretty between us."

"Alright, sounds like a plan," Khyree responded. "How you been, though? You've been so M.I.A, I hardly see you."

"You saw me last week, nigga," Hassan reminded him.

"I know, but I usually see you at least four times a week," Khyree explained. "I see someone's got your ass hella busy."

Hassan smiled before speaking, "Yeah... We've just been kickin' it like every single day."

"So I'm guessing shit is good between you two? She's no longer mad about what she saw you do that night?"

"Nah, she's cool," Hassan voiced casually. "Best believe Dominique spoke to her that night."

"She did? Saying what exactly?"

"That her treatment is working so well that's she gonna live longer."

"What?"

"Exactly that, my nigga," Hassan stated. "Some utter bullshit."

"It's bullshit?"

"Damn fuckin' right it is, ain't no way she's living longer than she has too."

"But let's say for example it's true, how are you going to handle that?" Khyree questioned seriously.

"It's not true, it won't ever be true."

"But if it is?"

"I'm leaving her then," Hassan declared.

"And she won't say shit? She knows quite a lot of shit. What we do, who we work with."

"I'll have to be the one to make sure she doesn't say anything and keeps her mouth shut then."

"There needs to be a serious conversation had. You need to prepare her for all this, make her come to terms with you not being with her anymore, providing for her."

Hassan deeply sighed before saying, "I'll still be providing for her. Sending her money. That should be enough to keep her mouth shut. You know how much she loves extremely expensive things."

"You're still going to need to have a conversation with her, bro," Khyree insisted. "Or things might just start moving pear shaped. Especially between you and Nazariah, and I know how bad you want to be with her."

"Man, she's the only person I want to be with. I don't even know how she managed to get a nigga feeling for her this deeply. I couldn't one-night stand her, I had to date her. Now I don't want to stop dating her ass or being with her. She makes me so happy, bro, I swear."

"I'm truly happy for you, San, but you know what you need to do for what you're building with Nazariah to work. You need to speak to Dominique."

All Hassan knew was, he wanted to be with Nazariah. He wanted to be able to whisk her out of that small condo of hers and take her to his big ass mansion, let her move all her shit in and stay with him. But that seemed impossible since Dominique was still in the picture.

She needed to go.

***

242

Khyree: *Thanks for the heads up Naz. Don't let her know a thing please.*

Nazariah: *I promise I won't.*

Thank God Hassan had freely given Khyree, Nazariah's number, enabling Khyree to contact her and ask her for some assistance in how he could win Amina over. The only option he could see himself doing was coming clean to her about how he felt and praying she did the same.

Nazariah had let Khyree in on Amina's whereabouts for the day, and he couldn't wait to see her. He was not allowing her to run away from him this time either. Like she was able to the night of Hassan's club opening, making sure that Khyree was unable to drop her home.

This time, he was getting her to be right where he wanted her. With him.

Khyree parked his G-Wagon in the pharmacy parking lot, while sitting patiently inside his car, waiting.

Amina quickly left the pharmacy, her head still looking down at her bright phone screen as she tried to re-book her Uber. The last one she had picked hadn't gone through and now she was forced to make another one.

Honk! Honk!

The sudden sound of a car honking made her look up from her device.

The navy blue G-Wagon that she could see ahead, was a beauty to her eyes. Never in her life had she ever seen a customized navy blue Mercedes Benz G-Wagon. And now that she was seeing it, she was truly in love.

But not in love with the man sitting comfortably in the driver's seat.

What the hell was he doing over here?

Amina figured the best thing for her to do would be to act like she hadn't seen him. Hopefully he would leave her alone.

Honk! Honk! Honk!

"Amina!"

Amina felt her heart skip a beat hearing his sexy baritone call out her name. He was adamant on trying to gain her attention, but she was adamant on ignoring him. She continued to stare down at her bright phone screen trying to see the status of her Uber. It had to be close by.

"Amina, you hear me callin' you."

And I'm trying my hardest to ignore you, nigga, she mused.

"Amina, please just get in. I really ain't in the mood for this," he told her in a much softer tone.

"Then maybe you should just go," she finally spoke to him, lifting her head from her phone. "No one's asking you to be here. You really need to stop stalking me."

"But I want to be here," he insisted. "I ain't stalkin' you, either. Nazariah let me know what your plans were for today."

Amina was suddenly confused and even more irritated. Why the hell had Nazariah done that?

"Just get in, Amina. Hear a nigga out and then you can go," he offered with a small grin.

Amina definitely wasn't in the mood for Khyree. She wasn't in the mood to hear what he had to say or play whatever game he was playing. But the fact that he had gone out of his way to find out what she was up today so that he could find her, had her a little gassed. She couldn't deny it.

Listening to him for a few minutes can't hurt, can it? she questioned herself.

Amina slowly walked to his passenger car door, opened it and got inside. The second she took a seat next to him, she felt her nerves fly through the roof. She didn't like the effect he had on her emotions so naturally and easily. Even just being in his presence right now was starting to drive her crazy, and the fact that his seductive scent was all around her, she felt like she was going to faint.

Khyree pulled off in front of the pharmacy, driving the car back onto the main road, and feeling very accomplished with the fact that Amina was sitting right next to him.

He found it hard to keep his eyes on the road and admire her at the same time, because all he really wanted to do was keep his eyes on her. He couldn't lie, she was looking good. Too good in fact, dressed in a white cami top, denim shorts and white Chuck Taylors on her feet. It was a simple outfit but it looked really nice on her. Almost too nice, and the more Khyree's eyes began to examine her, the more he realized how juicy those bare, long legs of hers were looking.

"You got somethin' to cover up in one of those bags of yours?" he questioned her with a serious facial expression.

"Huh?"

"You heard me," he said, not playing with her. "You got somethin' to cover up with? If not, I can go get you somethin' to cover up with."

246

"What the hell are you talking about, Khyree? What exactly do I need to cover up?"

"Those damn mothafuckin' sexy legs of yours," he snapped, stopping the car at a red light. "I ain't allowing niggas to be lookin' and fantasizing on shit that belongs to me."

Amina's eyes widened with surprise at his words. *Did he just say what I think he just said?* However, she quickly got over it and decided to go off on him. "Nigga, what belongs to you exactly?"

"I just told your dumb ass," he retorted. "Those legs."

"No they don't."

"Yeah they do," he responded, beginning to drive the car again now that the light had hit green.

"Uh-uh, they don't. And FYI, you ain't my daddy, so you can't tell me what I need to cover up on my body," she voiced boldly. "You're not the boss of me, Khyree."

"Is that so?" he taunted her playfully. "I ain't your daddy?"

Amina instantly rolled her eyes seeing the way he had taken the conversation. He had now turned her words in his head into something sexual.

"No," she fumed.

247

"Yeah, we gon' see 'bout that," he concluded before remaining silent and continuing to drive the car onto the freeway.

All Amina could do was follow suit and keep silent. She relaxed into his plush leather car seats and tried her hardest to stop thinking about how much she wanted to ride his face tonight. As much as he annoyed and frustrated her, she couldn't deny the way she felt towards him. She was definitely attracted to him.

Half an hour later, Khyree pulled up to an expensive looking restaurant that Amina had never been to before. It was only when she noticed the sign that she read *Benihana*.

Damn... This nigga did not just bring me to this expensive ass place!

She was actually quite happy he had whisked her away to grab a meal, because only the Lord knew how hungry she was right now. Just before Amina could reach for her seat belt, Khyree stopped her.

"You so eager to go eat, but you don't even wanna find out why a nigga brought you here in the first place?" he asked her with a light chuckle.

Amina simply shrugged before questioning, "Why did you bring me out here?"

"Because I want to get to know you, Amina," he admitted truthfully. "I like you and I know you like me too. If you don't like me, then tell me now and I'll promise I'ma leave you alone."

"I don't lik—"

"I'll smack the shit outta you," he threatened her.

Amina couldn't help but burst out in laughter at his sudden mood change. He was the one that told her to tell him she didn't like him, right? So why was he acting crazy now? Although Amina knew for a fact that she liked him, she just wasn't expecting for him to act so mean towards her saying that she didn't.

"You wouldn't dare," she amusingly stated. "I'll only end up smacking the shit out of you 10 times harder."

"And you wouldn't dare," he replied in a much calmer tone. "You were joking, right?"

"About what?"

"The bullshit you just tried to say about not likin' me."

Amina sighed before turning her head away from him. So she was no longer getting lost into those mesmerizing brown eyes of his. "Yes, I like you Khy—"

He never gave her a chance to finish though. Because as soon as he had heard the three words he had been dying to hear from her for so long, he pulled her chin towards him and pushed his lips onto hers.

Amina swore sparks flew.

He hadn't even given her a chance to get into it, he just went straight for the kill. The kill being her soft lips. Now they were kissing. Kissing with so much love, lust and passion mixed into one. Amina didn't understand why she hadn't kissed him before, because kissing him now felt wonderful. So wonderful that she didn't want to stop feeling his lips seduce her. But once he pulled away, she knew that it was over for now.

Amina's eyes gently fluttered open to stare at his handsome face that was now sporting a smirk.

"Knew you wanted a nigga from the jump," he happily commented, resulting in Amina to playfully hit his muscular bicep.

Seeing how good his muscles looked in a fitted blue shirt, his entire body in fact, was turning her on. Turning her on so much that she was considering risking it all for him tonight.

Khyree leaned into her lips once more, pecking them lightly before saying, "Let's go eat, beautiful."

***

"I do have a little time left Hassan, my doctors told me."

Hassan didn't usually believe a word that came out her mouth. But now, the way her eyes were filling with so much hope and joy had him worried. Was she telling the truth?

"How is that possible, D? You're in stage four pancreatic cancer," he reminded her. "Your cancer has spread. You're still going to die…"

"It's spread yes but the treatment can extend my life for a few more years, two at least," she explained.

"So the treatment could extend your life further than originally thought?"

She nodded. "Yes," Dominique voiced happily. "Well, not extend it amazingly but enough for me to live my life for the next two years of my life with you, baby. I love you so much and I really don't want to lose you anytime soon, Hassan." Dominique moved closer to him before grabbing hold of his hand. "We'll be able to finally start a family and be together some more before I go. The one thing I've always wanted to do for you is give you a child.." Then she planted a kiss onto his soft cheek. "I love you so much, Hassan."

All Hassan could do was remain still and listen to her. She

loved him, but he no longer loved her. The love he felt wasn't for her at all.

It was all for Nazariah Jordan.

$ CHAPTER SEVENTEEN $

You can do this, Nazariah. It's simple. You're just going to tell him it's over between you two. You don't want to be in a relationship with him anymore. It's not him, it's you. You're just not feeling this anymore.

Nazariah exhaled deeply as she chugged down her red wine. Once it was finished, she placed her wine glass on the table in front of her before picking up her cell and checking to see where he was.

You close?

She waited five minutes for a response, but nothing came. She waited another five minutes, but again, nothing came.

It wasn't until 20 minutes later that she finally received a response from him.

Anthony: *Sorry bae, stuck at work tonight. Can't see u anymore. Maybe tomorrow?*

Nazariah angrily threw her phone back onto the glass table and ran her fingers through her hair, trying to remain cool.

The one time she wanted to get serious and pluck up the courage to leave him was when he had to be busy. What utter bullshit.

Nazariah knew for a fact that she no longer wanted to be
Anthony. There was only one person she wanted to be with and it
most definitely wasn't him.

She could no longer stay in a relationship with him while
trying to start something with Hassan. They were becoming more
and more serious daily, and she was falling for him deeper and
deeper too. Much deeper than she had ever fallen for Anthony.

She needed to leave him.

Ding!

Nazariah's phone brightly lit up alerting her of a text
notification.

Hassan: *Coming over tonight. See you in a few, Miss Shyness.*

She couldn't help but smile at his message. She sure was glad
that he was coming over because she didn't want to spend tonight
in her bed alone.

Lately, she hardly slept alone because Hassan would often be
in her bed, right beside her, with his arms wrapped tightly around
her. She absolutely loved sleeping with him.

"Miss me?"

Nazariah sexily bit her lips at him, one hand on her open door as she carefully eyed him up and down. He was dressed casual but still looking very attractive in denim jeans, a black fitted short sleeved shirt and black J's on his feet.

"You know I did, baby," she whispered, pulling him into her apartment by his hand.

Hassan grinned, kicking her apartment door shut behind him and letting her lead him in, while his eyes fixated on her ass in those tight pink pajama shorts of hers. He already couldn't wait to get a taste of her tonight.

She led him past her living room, feeling his hand smack her butt just as they both entered her bedroom.

"Oww, San, that hurts," she shyly commented.

He chuckled before stating, "It hurts good though. You know you love me doin' that shit to you, Naz."

She cracked a smile as she turned to face him.

"Besides, with the way that ass of yours is starting to get fatter daily, I can't help but smack that juicy shit," he explained lustfully, grabbing hold of her butt and smacking it once more.

Nazariah's smile grew wider and she slightly lifted herself on her tippy toes so that she could brand her lips onto his.

"So what you wanna do tonight, baby?" Hassan queried just as their lips parted.

"Umm… It's pretty late, we can just watch Netflix," she suggested.

"And chill?" Hassan asked before smirking sexually at her.

"Uh-uh, wash those dirty thoughts out your mind boy. Just Netflix." Just when she tried to walk away from him, Hassan held her in place in front of him.

"What's wrong with us doing Netflix and chill?" he asked curiously. "We do the chillin' part almost every night anyways."

"Because I actually wanna watch a movie," she explained. "We'll chill after… Way, way, way after."

"A'ight," he agreed. "But don't fall asleep on a nigga because I'll wake your ass up and end up fuckin' you back to sleep."

Nazariah playfully rolled her eyes at him before heading to her en-suite bathroom. "I'll be out in a bit, get comfortable."

Hassan did as she said and lifted his shirt off his body. He was just happy to be with Nazariah tonight because he knew there was no way he could spend the night at that mansion with that deluded woman.

It was like she had forgotten all she had tried to do him before her cancer. Like she had forgotten who she used to be and what she used to do to people. Scamming them for their money and whatever else she could get her little hands on.

It didn't matter whether she had cancer or not, Hassan knew for a fact there was no way he could be with her. He had fallen out of love with her a very long time ago and there was going to be no chance for him to fall back in love with her. He was falling in love with someone else.

Nazariah stared at her reflection, breathing lightly as she remembered the one thing that she hadn't been able to do tonight.

Break up with Anthony.

It was killing her that she was still with him because all she wanted to do was be with Hassan. She knew that she needed to get it done sooner than later because if Hassan found out, she knew that he would go crazy. Even though that would make him a hypocrite as he was still with Dominique but still, he wouldn't give a shit. She knew how crazy he would blow up.

She needed to end things, ASAP.

***

"Come here... Why you tryna act all shy for?"

"I'm not shy. You see something you want? You come get it then."

All Khyree could do was continue to stare at her lustfully and keep both of his hands on his lap in front of him.

After their lunch date yesterday, things seemed to be going well between the both of them. They were quickly getting to know each other much better and enjoying each other's company. Enjoying each other's company so much that Amina let Khyree crash at her place for the night; on her couch, of course. She wasn't about to give up her body to him without letting him work hard for her. That's not the way things worked in her book.

Khyree kept silent but decided that he wanted his hands to do all the talking for him right now. He slowly reached over to Amina's thigh, gently beginning to stroke her soft, warm skin. She wanted him to come get what he wanted, then he was going to do exactly just that.

Amina stared at him staring at her. Those brown eyes filled with so much lust for her. She could tell how much he wanted her. He didn't even need to touch her for her to know, she just knew. And she knew that she wanted him just as bad.

"I know what I want, Amina," he whispered seductively to her. "Do you?"

Amina simply nodded, feeling his hand move higher up her thigh.

"You do?"

"I do," she whispered shyly.

"What do you want?" Khyree asked as he moved closer to her, still moving his hand higher up her thigh, reaching the middle of her legs.

"I want you, Khyree," she told him, looking as he leaned closer to her face.

"I know you do," he cockily answered before trying to lock their lips together.

"Nigga, please," Amina frowned, playfully pushing his face away.

"I want you too, beautiful," he stated with a chuckle. "I really do."

Amina grinned before letting him lock their lips together in a passionate, delicate kiss. As their lips perfectly meshed together, their hands began to fondle one another lovingly. Amina definitely didn't want this moment that had brewed between them to end.

Khyree suddenly pulled their lips apart, only to remove his

shirt off his body and the second it came flying off, Amina swore her heart stopped. His whole entire physique had been crafted to complete perfection and Amina wanted to do nothing more than caress all over his ripped, hot body.

Then he leaned back into her and pressed his lips back onto hers before beginning to caress her again.

Amina's arms wrapped around his neck, pulling him much closer towards her and continuing to kiss him. Their tongues romantically danced and collided with one another, the sexual tension between them both growing rapidly.

And just when Amina felt Khyree's hands begin to lift the bottom of her shirt, their time together was suddenly interrupted by The Game's rapping.

Khyree instantly groaned with annoyance before apologizing to Amina. "I'm sorry, beautiful, I gotta take this."

She nodded with a soft sigh.

"As soon as I'm done, I'm all yours again," he sweetly told her, giving her a quick peck before reaching for his phone in his back pocket.

"Yo, why the hell are you ringin' me right now? This better be for some really good shit..."

Amina patiently waited, admiring Khyree's handsome face while he spoke on the phone. She didn't think she could wait any longer. She believed she was giving it all to him tonight. That's how bad she wanted him.

"What the... Are you sure?!"

From his sudden change of tone and facial expression, Amina could tell that something was very wrong.

"I'm on my way. No, don't tell him. I'ma tell him or he'll only end up blowin' up. A'ight, bye."

And that their time together had been suddenly cut short.

"Beautiful, I got some shit to handle... I'm sorry, but I need to leave."

***

"I really don't believe this. No, I refuse to believe it. The Jamaicans get their shit stolen by you, our shit! Now you sittin' here telling me that you've lost our shit too!" Hassan raged, full of so much irritation because of the current situation.

The product that the Knight Brothers had just recently given to the Leones, had been stolen. The same way that the Jamaicans had been robbed by the Leones, the Leones had now magically lost their shit. And for Khyree and Hassan to say that they were angry

262

right now, would be an understatement.

"We don't know how it happened, jefe, it just did. I sincerely apologize."

Khyree banged loudly on the mahogany circle table in front of them. "Bullshit! You apologizing is not going to bring back the very large amount of product we gave you to sell. What the fuck do you mean you don't know what happened? You don't know who robbed you guys?"

Mario simply shook his head no.

"You don't know who robbed you?" Hassan decided to question him too.

"No," Mario said. "We really don't."

"Well, that's just absolutely fantastic," Hassan announced with a grin. "Absolutely fuckin' fantastic. Well, you and this 'we' you speak of, can take your stupid asses off my territory and start lookin' for someone else to work for."

"But jefe, it wasn't our fault! And you're the main dis—"

"You heard the man," Khyree cut him off. "Leave."

"But jefe, please, just he—"

Hassan interrupted him rudely, "Uh-uh, I don't want to hear

another word out your mothafuckin' mouth. You fucked up twice. First, when you stole from me and second, when you allowed my shit to get stolen. You should be dead right now, but you're lucky I'm in a good state of mind to let you leave here with a beating heart. I suggest you leave now before I suddenly change my mind, Mario."

Mario decided to keep his mouth shut and do as Hassan wanted. It was better he did that before he left here in a body bag. Mario just shot both Knight Brothers a menacing grin before walking out the room.

Hassan was completely done with him. He hadn't had the chance to have a conversation with Blaze yet about Mario, but there was absolutely no need now.

Mario could not be trusted.

Loving My Miami Boss

$ CHAPTER EIGHTEEN $

"Mmm," Nazariah gently moaned. "Hassan... Khy's right there."

Hassan reluctantly lifted his lips off her neck. "And so? That nigga don't care. He's in the front seat being hella salty right now."

"Umm, actually, I ain't salty, nigga... I care that Amina ain't in this car right now," Khyree declared, his face twisting up in a tight frown. "What the fuck is takin' her ass so long? We just going out to eat, the four of us. That's it. This ain't no fancy shit."

"See? What'd I say baby, he's salty," Hassan voiced with a chuckle before latching his lips back onto Nazariah's neck.

"Mmm... Khy, she'll be out in a second or two. She's just tryna look good for you," Nazariah told him, finding it slightly hard to concentrate with the way Hassan was trying to seduce her with his neck kisses. He always knew how weak they got her.

"If she's not out in five minutes, I'ma need you to get out and go get her, Naz," Khyree requested. "Cause if I do it, then shit won't be nice."

Nazariah looked out of Khyree's tinted window, hoping to see Amina step out her condo. She needed to hurry up because her man was getting mad waiting for her.

Nazariah was glad that they had both decided to stop playing games with each other and just be together. It was always evident from the start that they wanted each other.

It wasn't until a few seconds later that Amina stepped out, and Nazariah was pleased.

"See, Khyree, she's out!"

Khyree, on the other hand, wasn't pleased.

The second she sat shotgun right next to him and tried to move in for a kiss, Khyree instantly mushed her face away, shocking not just Amina, but Nazariah and Hassan who were in the back seats.

"Khyree, what the he—"

"Go change," he suddenly snapped.

"What?"

"I'm not 'bout to tell your ass a second time," he retorted, staring at the steering wheel instead of her. "Go fuckin' change."

"What the hell is wrong with you, Khyree?!" Amina yelled close to his face, pushing two fingers onto his forehead. "What is wrong with what I'm wearing?! Zariah, you see something wrong with what I'm wearing?" Amina turned to the back seat to stare at Nazariah and Hassan.

"I think you look great," Nazariah mumbled.

Amina did look great.

She was wearing a two-strap yellow dress that was quite short, but it showcased those lovely legs of hers. However, it had quite a low revealing neckline that was showing quite a lot of her cleavage.

"You really think I'm gon' let you go out with your ass, titties and legs out. You must be fuckin' stupid! Go and change, Amina, right now!"

"And you must be fucking stupid if you think I'm obeying you, Khy! I'm not changing."

"Then I guess we ain't goin' out to eat today. I told you before that you belong to me. I ain't lettin' other niggas stare freely at what belongs to me!" he fumed. "I don't know what other dumb, square niggas you been with before me, but just know I ain't nothing like them, Amina! This shit won't run while you're with me, so I'ma tell you this one more mothafuckin' time, go and fuckin' change."

"Clearly you're deaf and need to go seek some medical assistance because like I just said before, I ain't obeying your controlling, rude, light-skinned ass, Khyree. I ain't changing and that's that!"

While they continued to argue, Hassan discreetly told Nazariah to come with him into his car so they could get going separately to grab some grub. Going together as a group was no longer going to work.

Amina and Khyree had been arguing even before they got together, and Hassan and Nazariah were over it.

Hassan understood Khyree's frustrations right now though. If Nazariah had come out dressed like that, he would make her change too. Thank God she had opted for jeans today.

The Knight Brothers were protective and controlling over their women, and that's just the way shit was. But Hassan knew that Khyree had met his match. He would have to cool it, because the fact that Amina could take him on while he went crazy just showed that she was just as crazy as him. They were perfect for each other.

***

Nazariah reached over the table to wipe Hassan's lips that had been slightly stained with some of her red lipstick. They had had a full make out session before stepping out his Lambo, and it was evident on his lips.

Hassan smirked at her as she wiped her lipstick off his lips before turning to face his brother, once she was done.

Khyree had a mean mug on his face as he observed Amina sitting in front of him, tapping away on that phone of hers.

"You good, bro?" Hassan asked him amusingly, knowing fully well he wasn't good. He was just fucking with him now.

Despite convincing Amina to wear a cardigan to cover up all that cleavage she had going on, Khyree still wasn't happy. He hated the fact that she had disobeyed him and not changed. But at the same time, he secretly loved it.

"Fuck yes," he voiced through gritted teeth, still keeping his eyes fixed on Amina.

Hassan simply shook his head, trying his hardest to keep his laughter to himself and deciding to focus all his attention back on his baby. Khyree and Amina would soon be talking again, he already knew how they operated.

Hassan reached across the table for Nazariah's hands, intertwining their fingers together.

"Did I tell you how beautiful you look today, Miss Shyness?"

She shook her head yes before asking, "Did I tell you how handsome you look today, Mr. Knight?"

270

"You d—"

"Awww, you guys are so annoyingly cute," Amina cooed sweetly, looking up from her phone.

"Nazariah and Hassan shot her a happy smile each, and turned back to stare at one another again.

Amina got up out her seat but Hassan and Nazariah were too focused on each other to notice what she was up to.

Nazariah looked into those green eyes, swooning over how beautiful they were. She would never be able to get over them. She knew for a fact that this man right here had her heart. There was nobody else that had it now but him. She had fallen so quickly for him that she had now become addicted. Everything about Hassan Knight she was in love with.

Hassan felt exactly the same way. He could see himself being with her for a very long time. She was the perfect woman for him. Sexy as fuck, loyal and educated. She was everything he could ever want and more.

"I just want a kiss Khy."

"Nah, leave me alone. I'm still mad at your ass."

"I want a kiss," Amina pleaded, lifting his chin up towards her. She had gotten out her seat and came to stand next to where

Khyree was sitting.

He was still angry with her but trying to resist her was just becoming harder and harder. He couldn't resist the touch of her lips on his. And even though he was trying his hardest to dodge her kisses, he wanted to kiss her. So he eventually gave in, kissing her back but still frowning at her.

"Thank you, baby," Amina said calmly, kissing the side of his smooth face before heading back to her seat in front of him. On her face was a large toothy smile revealing her white teeth.

Just when Amina sat back down, Nazariah's phone began to vibrate and even though she had put it on silent, that hadn't stopped the vibrations.

Zing! Zing! Zing!

Nazariah reached for her phone but Hassan beat her right to it.

Shit.

"Who the hell is this?"

She had managed to glance at the caller I.D. before he snatched her phone off the table.

It was Anthony.

"Why the hell is this nigga still callin' you? Ain't you ended shit with him?" Hassan questioned her suspiciously, throwing her phone back on the table.

"I've been trying to," she admitted nervously. "But every time I try, he's always busy and I—"

"You don't *try* to break up with someone, Naz, you just do it."

"Well, every time I try to do it, he's not available."

"You don't need to see the nigga face to face," Hassan instructed her firmly. "Just send him a text and tell him it's over between you two. Simple."

"I can't just do that, Hassan. We've been off and on for two years. I owe him an expl—"

"You don't owe that nigga shit!" he yelled, his fists suddenly clenching and his jaw tightening.

He was starting to create a scene. People around them were now staring at their direction with looks of disapproval.

"Hassan, I can't just break up with him over text," she informed him gently.

"Yes, you can and you will," he fumed. "Matter fact, you don't need to do it, I'll do it for you since you're finding that shit so hard to do all of a sudden."

"I'm not finding it hard!" Nazariah protested. "I just want to be able to have a face to face conversation with him and explain why I'm breaking up with him."

"And I'm telling you that you don't need to do all that shit. Is your ass suddenly retarded and not listening to a nigga? Send him a damn text!"

Nazariah wasn't about to go back and forth with Hassan right now, not with others they didn't know in earshot of their disagreement.

She decided that the best idea for her would be to just leave. She grabbed her purse, phone, and just when she got up out her seat to leave, a hand grabbed her arm.

"And where the fuck do you think you're going? Sit your ass back down, Nazariah."

"Get off me," she spat, clawing at his fingers which made him instantly wince with pain.

Nazariah stormed out the restaurant, determined to catch an Uber and get home as soon as possible.

She had had enough of Hassan today.

Once outside, she began to browse through her phone, looking for the Uber app. And just when she clicked on it, she felt a strong hand grip onto her arm.

"What the... Hassan! Let me go!" she protested, but it was no use.

Hassan still continued to drag her towards the parking lot where his car was parked. When they had arrived by his car, he unlocked his Lambo with a touch of his button and his red doors went flying up.

"Get the fuck in before I make you get in," he ordered bossily at Nazariah, letting go of her arm so she could do what he wanted.

Once she had reluctantly gotten inside, Hassan followed suit, pulling his car door down when he was comfortably in.

All was silent, as they both sat inside.

Nazariah refused to speak to him and he refused to speak to her. She just didn't get why he was overreacting about Anthony. She knew that if he had found out, he would, but now that it had happened, she found it stupid.

Hassan, on the other hand, found it stupid that she was still with Anthony. She still had that nigga believing that she belonged to him, when she really belonged to Hassan.

"I'm sorry about blowing up on you like that, Naz." Hassan decided to put his pride aside and stop being stubborn. He didn't like not being in a good place with Nazariah. It made him very uncomfortable.

"I guess I was just jealous... That you're still with him."

Nazariah reached for his chin so that he was forced to now stare at her. "You have nothing to be jealous about, Hassan. I'm with you now, aren't I? You're with me basically every night, the only man I give my body to. I'm not trying to put off breaking up with him, he's the one that's always unavailable. But I promise you that I will break up with him as soon as I can," she explained lovingly.

"But I don't get why you can't break up with him over te—"

"No," she said, cutting him off.

"Just one simple te—"

"No," she repeated. "I need to do this face to face, Hassan, please. Just trust me on this one."

Hassan simply nodded before turning his head back towards the front window. He didn't know what else to say. If she wanted him to just trust, her then he guessed he would just have to do that.

Nazariah kept quiet and still, watching Hassan as he stared ahead. She knew he still wasn't happy about her wanting to have a conversation with Anthony, but she knew he would get over it. The same way she was getting over him being married.

Nazariah slowly lifted a hand to his thigh, before gently beginning to stroke it, moving higher up his thigh.

Hassan looked down with curiosity at her hand on him before looking up at her. The want for him was clearly evident in those pretty eyes of hers. And having tinted car windows meant that they would not be disturbed if they wanted to get shit popping right now.

Nazariah's hand had finally reached its goal and when she landed on his crotch, she let her hand rest on his growing erection for a minute.

"Naz..."

She got off her seat so she could move closer to Hassan and sit frontwards on him.

"Yes, baby?" she queried, her voice drunk with love and lust for him.

"Right now?" he asked, wanting to make sure that this is what she wanted.

Nazariah's arms wrapped around his neck and she sank herself lower onto his hardness.

"Right now," she whispered, kissing the side of his neck as his hands squeezed her butt.

"You sure?"

"Yes, Hassan. I want you, right now," she reassured him.

And once that reassurance came, Hassan no longer held back. She wanted him to fuck her in his car, then he was going to do just that.

Nazariah felt herself being lifted off Hassan and pushed down onto her seat, with her back touching the plush leather.

The freak in him had finally awoken.

"San..."

All she could do was lay back with excitement as he quickly unzipped her jeans and pulled them down her legs. Her purple thong was next to go but instead of pulling them down, Hassan eagerly ripped them off.

"Those were my favorite," Nazariah voiced with a sad pout.

"I'll buy you a new one," Hassan stated with a sexy grin, stroking her warm thighs. "A whole bunch of fuckin' sexy new ones."

Nazariah happily nodded, biting her lips at him before lifting

278

her back off her seat so she was face to face with him again.

Their lips joined and hungrily began to kiss, desperate for a taste of one another. While they kissed, Nazariah's hands went straight for his pants, unzipping and pushing them down.

Five minutes later, Nazariah swore she was seeing stars.

"Uhhhhh, shit."

It's not fair what he did to her. Providing her constantly with so much passion, pleasure and pain all at the same damn time, and still making her want him even more.

"Hassan... please," she begged.

It was like he was trying to kill her with that incredibly, amazing dick of his. With each quick thrust inside her, Nazariah felt like her mind was going to explode.

"Please, what?"

"Too much," she managed to make out just as he pushed his thick rod deeper inside her. She could feel herself creaming all over him.

"You can take it," he groaned passionately.

"Ugh, no," she disagreed. He was definitely trying to break her. The faster he fucked her, the more it hurt. The more it hurt so damn good. But she wanted a chance to take a break for a minute, a second at least. "Agh! Hassan, let's sto—"

"We're not stoppin', girl," he announced, still pounding deeper and deeper, in and out of her. "This your dick, you can take it."

"I-I can't," she whimpered, clawing her nails into his arms.

"You can," he insisted firmly, his large size still moving in and out of her tight pussy. "Take every last inch of this dick, baby."

All Nazariah could do was what he wanted and continue to take his bomb ass dick.

***

Nazariah snuggled up closer to him on her bed as they passionately kissed. Her fingers ran through his soft curls while his hands gently fondled her breasts.

Today has definitely been an eventful day. Filled with heated arguments, deep conversations and some mind blowing car sex.

But through it all, Hassan and Nazariah managed to grab some lunch with Amina and Khyree and just enjoy one another's company.

Now, Nazariah and Hassan were back at her place, cuddling and kissing together in bed.

Nazariah didn't want this sweet moment between them to end. Kissing him always felt amazing to her. It was one of her favorite things to do.

Ring! Ring! Ring!

Determined to keep on focusing on Nazariah, Hassan tried his hardest to block out his ringing phone on the lamp stand opposite him. But shit was pretty hard when it just kept on going off.

Ring! Ring! Ring!

Nazariah slowly pulled her lips off his, making Hassan groan with annoyance.

"I don't want to answer it, Naz," he announced, already reading her thoughts.

"Just answer it, baby. I'm not going anywhere."

Hassan sighed deeply before reaching for his phone and looking at the caller I.D. only to see Dominique's name on his screen. Ever since seeing the look on Nazariah's face back in the Dominican, when she saw "Wife" in his phone, he decided to change it to Dominique's actual real name.

Even without her being here, she had managed to ruin his time with Nazariah.

"What?" he rudely answered.

"Sir, it's me, Jayde."

Jayde was Dominique's nurse that Hassan had hired to look after her. She had never called him up before.

"What's up?"

"It's Mrs. Knight... She's collapsed."

Loving My Miami Boss

$ CHAPTER NINETEEN $

Hearing that Dominique had collapsed, suddenly made Hassan panic with fear. Even though he no longer loved her and wasn't very nice to her most of the time, he still cared about her. So imagine his surprise when he rushed home, leaving Nazariah only to see Dominique, perfectly fine, sitting on the carpeted living room floor browsing a wedding dress magazine.

It had all been a ploy.

A ploy to get him to leave whatever he was doing and come straight to her. Dominique hadn't fallen at all. She was perfectly fine!

"Why the hell would you make your nurse call me and say that you've collapsed?" Hassan asked, full of irritation. "What the fuck is wrong with you?! You made me leave what I was doin', to come straight to your stupid ass."

"Well, it worked, didn't it?" she smiled happily, taking a sip of her wine glass. "You're here. Right where you're supposed to be."

"I don't believe this shit right now," Hassan snapped. "You're a fool for this!"

"I'm a fool in love with you," she responded. "Wish you could say the same, but it seems like you've seem to have forgotten

284

where home is."

"And what's that supposed to mean?"

"Exactly what I just said. You seem to have forgotten where home is," she stated coolly, flicking to the next page of her magazine. "I'm over here looking for a new dress for me to renew our wedding vows in..."

Renew their wedding vows? She must have been losing her mind. Hassan was never going to marry her, ever again. She didn't even deserve to have his last name right now.

"...But you're the one out here, cheating on me."

All Hassan could do was remain silent. What was the point of lying or hiding the fact that he no longer wanted her? If she had put two and two together, then great. It's about time she found out.

"You're not even denying it, Hassan!" she yelled, her eyes welling up with tears. "You're cheating on me, aren't you?! Tell me the truth right now!"

"I've met someone else, yes," he admitted. "And I'm in love with her."

Dominique loudly began to wail out in pain, chucking her magazine far away from her.

"You're lying! You're lying! You're lying! Please tell me you're lying Hassan, please!" She screamed, her tears cascading down her now red cheeks.

"I ain't lyin', D," he nonchalantly informed her. "I've been seeing someone else for over a month now. I don't want this marriage anymore. I still want to pro—"

"No! No! No—"

"—to provide for you, but I no longer want to stay married to you. And that's the honest truth."

"No!" Dominique yelled, getting up to run towards him. When she was in front of him, she looked up at him with tears still falling down her cheeks. "You can't leave me, Hassan, I love you!"

"Well I don't love you, D," he voiced. "And that's just the way it is."

"Please, Hassan," she begged, holding onto him in the hopes of trying to convince him. "Please don't leave me. We're supposed to be together forever. I love you."

"No, Dominique. I don't love you."

***

Nazariah took one glance at Anthony's pissed off facial

expression and simply rolled her eyes. She really didn't have time for this.

"You've gotta be kidding me right now. Please tell me that this is a joke, Nazariah. You're not breaking up with me."

"It's not a joke," she said. "I'm really breaking up with you, Anthony. I've been trying to do it for a while, but you're always so busy. Like I said before, it's not you, it's me."

"Bullshit!" he shouted, his face tightening up with anger. "You must be fucking somebody else. That's why you want to end things all of a sudden. Who is he?"

"I'm not sleeping with anyone else," she lied.

"Yes you are! We haven't had sex in months. The only explanation I can think of is because someone else is dicking you down. Who is he?"

"Anthony, I've told you my reasons for wanting to break up with you. If there's nothing else for you to say, then I think it's best you leave."

"I ain't going nowhere," he snapped. "Until you tell me who is fucking you. Who is it? Is it someone I know?"

"Anthony," Nazariah called, getting up from her sofa. "It's time you left."

"Who is it, Nazariah?! Who is fucking you behind my back?!" he yelled, getting up and towering over her.

"No one you need to worry about!" she yelled back. "Now just leave!"

"I don't believe this shit. You're a bitch for sitting there lying to my face, telling me that you don't want to be in a relationship with me, when you're clearly starting one with someone else!"

Nazariah scoffed with shock. Anthony had never called her a bitch before. "I'm a bitch?"

"Yes bitch, you're a bitch. I fucking love you!"

"Who you calling a bitch, bitch? Get out of my house! It's over between us, Anthony. I'm done talking to you."

"Oh yeah? Well I ain't done talking to you, Nazariah! How can you try and end things between us? After all that we've been through! I introduced you to my parents."

"I never wanted to meet your patents, Anthony! I only agreed because I felt guilty that you were getting upset because I didn't want to meet them."

"So you never wanted to meet them?" he questioned her in a tone filled with hurt.

"No, Anthony," Nazariah truthfully revealed. "I never wanted to meet them because meeting them would have given you false hope, thinking that we were getting serious. That something bigger was going to happen between us. When really, I just didn't want to be with you anymore."

"Damn... So that's it? So that's how you feel?"

"That's how I feel," she concluded honestly.

When Anthony had finally gotten the message and decided to leave Nazariah alone, she realized that she wanted to speak to her best friend right now. She wanted to tell her that she had finally broken up with Anthony. She wanted to tell her how she had felt a sudden relief flow through her, like a burden had been lifted off her back.

She felt free.

"Hey, girl. What's up?" Amina picked up on the third ring.

"Hey," Nazariah drawled, noticing her instant distant tone. "I just called to talk."

"Oh, okay," Amina gently answered. "Anything in particular?"

"I broke up with Anthony."

"Uh-uh, Khy, stop... Naz, what did you say? You broke up

with Anthony?"

"Yeah," she said.

"About time! How'd he take it?"

"Well… At first he believed it was a joke but I managed to convince him otherwise. He finally got the message that I no longer wanted to be with him. He automatically guessed that I was seeing someone else though. Even though I still tried to convince him otherwise, he still figured it out. So now we're over and I feel so free. And I definitely think we should celebrate, just us two. How does that sound?"

"That sounds… Shit, uhh… Really good," Amina moaned.

"Amina? Something wrong?"

"Khyree, later," Amina mouthed to him. But it was no use, he will still adamant on getting her off the phone. He continued to hungrily kiss on her skin, knowing exactly how he was making her feel.

"Mmm, Naz, I'ma call you back, girl. Promise," Amina concluded before hanging up on Nazariah. "Khyree, I told you later."

"And I… told you now," he whispered in between his kisses on her neck. "I've been cravin' you all day."

"Is that so?"

"Yes..."

"Can I ask you something before we start?"

Khyree came up from her neck and looked at her strangely. "What's that?"

"What are w—"

He immediately cut her off already seeing where her question was heading. "You my girl, I'm your nigga. End of. Take those panties off."

Amina couldn't help but giggle. "Khyree, you didn't even let me finish."

"Cause I already know what you gon' ask me and I just answered it for you. We're together."

"We are?"

"Are you deaf?" he questioned her and sucked his teeth. Amina simply smiled, filled with so much joy. "We're together, beautiful. And that's all that matters."

Amina couldn't complain.

This time last year, she was all alone. With no handsome,

wealthy man to whisk her by her feet and drive her crazy. She had no one to love, no one to argue with, and no one to create intimate memories with.

"Uhh, Khyree…baby."

Now she had all of that and more.

Khyree's hands grabbed onto her long legs, pulling them both closer onto his torso so that he could push even deeper into her tight cave.

His lips kissed all over her face, trying to show her all the love and affection he had for her. There was no doubt about it, he had fallen for her.

"Khyree," Amina continued to moan, rubbing her hands on top of his muscular shoulders, feeling his lips go down her lips, down her throat, and down her naked chest.

The more she called his name, the more encouraged he felt to keep thrusting in and out of her. While he moved in and out of her at a steady speed, his lips made their way onto one of her chocolate tip nipples and eagerly latched on.

Amina's mind was completely blown as she felt his dick inside her and his soft lips make love to her nipples. Everything felt so damn good. His hard shaft pushing in and out of her, his lips swirling, licking and sucking away on her nipples. It all felt so good that she never wanted it to end.

"Oh Khy…"

Why was she so beautiful?

Khyree had to take a moment to just tower over her and just look at how beautiful she was to him. The more he stared into those pretty honey brown eyes of hers, the more infatuated he found himself becoming with her.

She was so damn beautiful to him.

Just looking on at the looks of pleasure that were sweeping across her face because of the way he was making love to her right now, brought an indescribable feeling to him. A feeling that he never wanted to lose.

He never wanted to lose her.

Khyree kept his eyes locked onto hers, keeping himself still inside her momentarily. And the shit he said next shocked the hell out of him.

"Amina, I love you."

MISS JENESEQUA

$ CHAPTER TWENTY $

~ Three Months Later ~

Hassan's eyes lit up with happiness as he watched his gorgeous girl step out of her hospital building and walk towards his car. He unlocked the doors for her from the inside, watching as her passenger side door flew up into the air.

Nazariah stepped in, pulling his car door down as she took a seat next to him.

"Hey, baby," she greeted him before moving in closer to his lips to lovingly kiss him. "Missed you."

"Missed you too, Miss Shyness," he informed her with a sexy smirk before starting his car engine. He hadn't seen her in four days and even though that might not have seemed that long, it was long for Hassan.

"How you've been without me?" he curiously asked.

"I've been okay, mostly grinding," she answered, lifting a hand to stroke the side of his face. "How about you?"

"Same, just been grindin' and thinking 'bout you," he admitted, leaning close to her lips and lightly pecking them.

"So what's our plans for today?" she curiously questioned.

"Well," he began, one hand gripping her thigh while the other worked the steering wheel. "I'ma take you home to get dressed out your work clothes and then I'm treating you for some lunch. How does that sound?"

"Sounds good," Nazariah responded with a large smile.

"What would you like to eat? Anythin' in particular?"

"You," she voiced seductively.

"Girl, now ain't the time for you to get all freaky on me," Hassan playfully snapped at her.

"Why? You asked me what I wanted," she reminded him shyly.

"There's over 50 cars behind us," Hassan informed her, making Nazariah look out the window to see that they were now on the freeway. "And your dumb ass already tryna make a nigga go crazy. I can't fuck you while we're on the freeway, girl. So just sit there, shut up and keep lookin' pretty."

Nazariah giggled lightly before announcing, "I definitely missed your rude ass."

Hassan flashed her a toothy grin before chuckling and focusing back on driving.

Once they arrived at her apartment, Hassan waited in the car while Nazariah changed out of her work clothes. Then when she was dressed and ready to head out for their lunch date, he drove them both to their desired destination.

They arrived at the restaurant, hand in hand, and were led to a private area of the fancy restaurant that was sealed off to the rest of the public. Their white table had red, white and pink rose petals neatly scattered all around it, red candles placed on top of the table, with white plates, a bucket of champagne, red champagne glasses, and a red rose on one of the plates.

"Aww, San," she cooed sweetly at him. "This is so romantic. All this for me?"

"All this for you, baby," he lovingly replied, lifting her hand to his lips. He planted a soft kiss on it, keeping his green eyes on her as he did so.

Nazariah immediately walked towards the plate with the red rose and took a seat. Hassan followed suit, taking a seat right in front of her.

It was only 10 minutes later once they had ordered their starters and gotten comfortable, that Hassan thought this was the right time to bring out what he had for her.

Nazariah was too busy looking at her phone to even notice the black jewelry box that Hassan had brought out from underneath their table. But she definitely noticed when he opened it towards her.

The silver diamond necklace with a heart locket was absolutely stunning. Nazariah felt her eyes watering up just looking at it. It was unlike anything she had ever seen this close before. It looked extremely expensive and precious. Almost too precious for her to touch.

"Hassan… That can't be for me," she blurted out nervously.

"Who the hell else would it be for?" he queried in a firm tone. "I bought it for you, Naz."

Nazariah remained speechless as she admired the necklace. She didn't know what to say or how to really act. No one ever bought her expensive things.

"Unless you don't want it? I can always return it."

"No, no, I do want it," Nazariah tried to reassure him. "I promise I do, it's just so beautiful and I… Thank you."

"You welcome, baby," he coolly stated. "You gon' let me put it on you?"

Nazariah willingly nodded before standing up and leaving her seat. Hassan left his seat, gently picking the necklace out its casing

298

before holding it delicately in his big hands.

Nazariah turned around and pushed her hair to the side, raising it slightly so that Hassan wouldn't have anything in the way while putting it on her.

He admired the way her attractive body looked in that baby pink sundress of hers, biting his lips and imagining all the things he couldn't wait to do to her tonight. He then stepped forward and kissed the back of her neck, before lifting the necklace above her head and bringing it down to her neck.

When Nazariah felt him clasp the necklace, she swore she had fallen in love with the piece of jewelry once more. Looking down at it only brought her so much overwhelming joy.

"Hassan, it's so beautiful," she announced, touching the heart and admiring its pretty design.

"Just like you," he whispered lightly into her ear. "Naz..."

"I really love it. Thank you so much," she continued to thank him, still admiring it.

"Naz, I love you."

Hassan had been wanting to tell her that for a very long time. Now that he was finally saying it, he felt an abundance of relief and satisfaction flow through him. He didn't care that he had been

299

the one to say it first and he definitely didn't care if she didn't say it back. He just really wanted to let her know.

"I love you too, Hassan."

***

He loves me! He really loves me.

Nazariah was still on cloud nine after her lunch date with her man. And him presenting her with a stunning, expensive gift and then telling her that he loved her had her over the moon. She was beyond pleased. But even with how pleased she was, she was still quite disheartened.

And as she lay peacefully on her king sized bed, watching Hassan strip his top off his body followed by his jeans, her disheartened state grew.

"What's up, Naz?"

It was as if he could read her mind without her even needing to tell him anything. That's just how well they clicked together.

"What?"

"C'mon," he said, rolling his eyes at her and slowly walking towards the edge of her bed. He was completely shirtless and only wearing his white boxers, and Nazariah's mind was about to go crazy watching that large dick print of his. She was becoming wet just looking at his fine self. "I know when something's up with you. Stop tryna front. What's wrong?"

She sat up once his palms wrapped around her ankles, shifting her down her bed. "Tell me what's wrong," he demanded, shifting her so that her legs were now hanging off the bed and he was looking straight down at her pretty face.

"I love you, you love me, but that's not all I want for us," she revealed.

"And what is it that you want?"

"I want us to get in a serious, deep relationship," she began.

"We are in a serious, deep relationship."

"Without you being married," she finished.

Hassan sighed before speaking, "We've talked 'bout this, Naz. I'm only with her because of her cancer. I'm basically waitin' for her to die."

"Well, stop waiting and get it together, San," she instructed with a frown. "I want us to be together, properly. I want to be able to meet your family and for you to meet mine. I want to be able to make plans to move in with you... Start something real."

"Whoa, baby, where is this all comin' from? We've started something real. From the second I saw you in the Dominican, we started something real."

"You're still married, Hassan," she reminded him sadly. "I don't want to spend the rest of this year waiting for your wife to die. That's not the kinda person I am."

"You don't need to wait for her to die, Naz, I'm the one waiting."

"How am I not waiting? That's what we're waiting for, together!" she suddenly shouted.

"Quit with the yellin', Naz," he warned, grabbing her chin. "You want to move in with me? Is that what you want? You want to meet my family? I can make all that ha—"

"No Hassan, I want you to no longer be married. I've tolerated it now for too long, but I'm no longer doing it. I don't want to be second best anymore."

"Who said you were second best, Nazariah? I told your ass that I love you today and before today, I've showed you every day that I love you, only you, girl. So what the fuck are you talkin' about sayin' you second best. You've never been second best!"

"I feel like I'm second best," she muttered.

"Well you ain't," he voiced, crouching down in between her legs and gently pushing her shoulders down. "I love you. I'm not gonna stop loving you. Ever."

"But Hassan, I'm worr—"

"Stop worrying," he ordered, slowly pulling her pink thong down her legs. "The woman I love doesn't need to worry about a damn thing because I've got her."

"But Hassan, I'm worried be—"

"What the fuck did I just tell you about worrying?" he rudely asked her, spreading her thighs apart so he could give himself the perfect access to her pearl. "Stop it, Nazariah."

"I'm worried because I feel like you're never going to leave her and she won't ever die," Nazariah quickly blurted out. "I'm worried becau... Uhh, Hassan!"

Hassan was no longer paying attention to anything she was saying. His only motive right now was to make her feel good.

"I love you," he whispered, pushing two fingers into her tightness. "That's all you need to worry about, baby." And before she could try and respond, Hassan latched his tongue onto her clit and began to devour her like she was the only food he needed to survive another day on this earth.

$ CHAPTER TWENTY-ONE $

"Khyree, please just talk to him for me, please. You're brothers, he'll listen to you."

"And what exactly do you expect me to tell him, Dominique?"

"That he can't leave me, we're supposed to be together," Dominique voiced in a tone filled with so much desperation. "I really love him, Khyree. I really don't want to lose him to whatever bitch he's fucking around with behind my back these days."

"But you can't force him to stay with you," Khyree informed her. "If he's no longer in love with you then I'm sorry, but you're just gonna have to accept it, Dominique."

"I won't accept it! He's my husband. We're meant to be together. I lo—"

"Dominique, stop it," Hassan cut across her suddenly, stepping into the living room that Khyree had been waiting for him in. "You're just embarrassing yourself right now. So stop it. We ain't meant to be together, things were never going to work out. I'm sorry it had to happen while you were going through this illness but it's over between us."

Dominique simply stared at Hassan with a blank facial

expression.

"I've already got my attorney setting up the papers as we speak," he stated. "I still want to be able to provide for you and ensure that you continue to receive top medical assistance, but this marriage is no longer happening."

Hearing Nazariah tell him the way she felt about him still being married, definitely left Hassan feeling some type of way. The fact that she was worried about it, had him worried about it, and quite frankly, he didn't want that. He didn't want that for them. For them to always have a burden on their relationship. So he had to what was best. What he really wanted.

Surprisingly, Dominique wasn't taking Hassan's words as badly as he thought she wouldn't. She wasn't hysterically crying or screaming, she was just looking at him with no emotion whatsoever. He took that as her finally getting over them and accepting the fact that their marriage was no more.

"Yo, Khyree, let's bounce," Hassan concluded before exiting the living room.

Today, Hassan and Khyree had a very important meeting with the connect. It was to discuss some new shipment coming in from the south and a new potential business opportunity. The Knight Brothers were distributors of narcotics but they dabbled in other things from time to time. That included the distribution of weapons and The Knights were looking to dabble in it again. This time more intensely and seriously.

While Hassan drove, Khyree fiddled around with the AUX cord, trying to connect it to his iPhone.

"Nigga, hurry up," Hassan retorted. "It don't take that long to connect your damn phone to the fuckin' cable."

"Yo, what's up with all this animosity?" Khyree asked with a hearty laugh.

"You're distractin' me. You know I don't like stuff going on while I'm driving, man. Hurry up."

"Sorry, old man," Khyree teasingly apologized, knowing how his brother got when it came to his driving. He loved to be careful. Khyree quickly plugged the AUX cord into his phone before scrolling through his music library. "Yo, so you really endin' things with D?"

Hassan nodded. "It's over between us. Been over for a long time but I just let shit slide because of her illness, but not anymore."

"What made you change your mind?"

"Nazariah," Hassan revealed. "She's worried Dominique might

not die as quick as we thought and I won't ever leave her. In her mind, she believes she's second best."

"Second best? Nah, you ain't ever treated a female the way you treat her. You really love her."

"I know, I know," Hassan agreed. "I finally told her that too."

"Oh word? Your mean ass told her you love her?"

"Yup," Hassan said with a smile. "Told her first, too."

"Wow!" Khyree exclaimed with surprise. "I honestly don't believe this. Hassan Knight tells a girl he loves her first... wow."

"Please, like you ain't told some girl you love her. I bet you already told Amina that shit."

"...Well, yeah, I did."

"You did?" Hassan questioned him with an arched brow, not really sure if he was being truthful or not. "When?"

"Three months ago when I was hittin' it," he explained. "I told her that I love her."

"And what'd she say?"

"She didn't say nothing."

"Wait, what?"

"She didn't say anything. So we kept it moving and pretended like it never happened. I said it too soon anyways."

"Nah, nigga, you said it just right," Hassan told him. "She probably just never expected it. There's no way that she don't love you back. I hope you ain't thinkin' that either."

"I don't know... I was hoping she would say it back some other time, but she still ain't. A nigga tryna not let it get to me but it's starting to have me a little on edge. What if she doesn't love me and I've just been playing myself the whole time, San?"

"You're a fuckin' idiot if you believe that shit," Hassan berated him. "Just cause she ain't said it yet don't mean that she doesn't love you, Khy. Give her a little more time to come around. Before you know it, she'll say it."

"Did Naz tell you she loves you too when you said it?"

Hassan nodded before adding, "But that still don't mean Amina don't love you. Every woman is different, bro. I've been reading so—"

Khyree suddenly laughed. "You've been reading, nigga? You can read?"

Hassan threw him a dirty look before cutting his eyes at him. "I've been reading some book and it was talking about how every woman is different. Just because one woman behaves one way, doesn't mean the next woman will do exactly the same. Women are like flowers. You need to study them, care for them, and be patient with them. They can't just grow over night. It's gonna take a while but if you're patient enough to stick around, they'll be worth the wait."

"That's some real cute ass, corny shit bro," Khyree chuckled. "But I get what you're saying one-hundred percent. I just need to be more patient, I guess."

Hassan shook his head in agreement as he kept his eyes on the road ahead. They were getting closer to their destination. Only a few minutes away.

"Mario was pretty pissed about us cutting him and his squad off like that," Khyree announced. "But he hasn't tried anything, so that's good."

"Yeah, and I know for a fact he hasn't found anyone else to supply him with drugs to sell. I've spoken to Sharif, Lamont and Scooter. They won't be givin' him any product to sell either. So he's not only cut from us, he's cut from any other plugs. He'll soon get the fuck outta Miami and go somewhere else."

"Bet."

"And I spoke to Blaze, too, about why he kicked The Leones out of ATL. Turns out they were greedy, terrors, and stealing from him on the low. Started a fuckin' gang war, almost killing Blaze's girl and their unborn kid."

"Damn," Khyree commented. "No wonder the fool had so much confidence to come steal from us in the first place. And if he ever came near Amina, I would kill him on sight. I don't know how Blaze managed to have the strength to spare his life."

"Yeah, exactly. He better just stay the fuck away because the next time I see him, I'll be sending a bullet through his brain," Hassan voiced seriously. "Real talk."

***

"You think you're what?!"

"I think I'm pregnant, girl," Amina whispered sadly. "Khyree's always wanting to have sex when he sees me. Sometimes even four times a damn night."

"Four times?" Nazariah questioned her amusingly through the phone. "That's even more than Hassan and I. You guys are such freaks."

"And we don't use condoms."

"But I thought you were on the pill, Amina? We get them

311

together."

"I am," Amina stated. "Well, I guess I am, sometimes."

"Sometimes? Amina, really?"

"Yeah," she responded innocently. "I sometimes forget."

"And this is why your ass is now pregnant."

"Could be pregnant," Amina corrected her. "I've only taken one test. I'm booking an appointment with the doctor."

"You're a nurse, Mina," Nazariah reminded her. "You know the symptoms. Stop playing. You're pregnant, aren't you?"

"…Yeah," Amina sheepishly answered. "I believe I am."

"Damn," Nazariah replied with a soft sigh. "You told Khyree yet?"

"No."

"Why not?"

"I don't know how he's gonna take it. We've only been together for three months and I think he's still a bit mad at me because I never told him I love him when he said it first."

"Huh? Wasn't that like ages ago? You still haven't told him yet?"

"Nazariah!" Amina whined. "I don't want to feel pressured into it.

"And who the hell is pressuring you to do anything? Just tell the man you love him!"

"I will in my own ti—"

Knock! Knock! Knock!

Three loud knocks suddenly sounded upon Nazariah's front door. Her first thought was Hassan but then she realized he now had a key to her apartment. He could just come in whenever he liked. So if it wasn't him, then who on earth was it?

"Amina, I'll be right back. Someone's at my door."

"Alright, girl," Amina concluded before ending the phone call.

Nazariah put her phone on the arm rest of her couch before getting up and stretching. Then she slowly sauntered to her front door and looked through the peephole.

Seeing his face immediately made her blood boil.

"Open up, Naz."

She sucked her teeth and rolled her eyes, keeping still in her place.

"Go away, Anthony," she snapped angrily. "I don't want you around here anymore."

"Well, I want to be arooooound!" he yelled. "Let me innnn."

"You've been drinking, Anthony," she said, noticing the drunken state he was in. "Go home."

"I'm not going anywhere until you let me in," he ordered, banging on her door with his fists. "I want to be with you tonightttt. Just the way we've always been."

"No Anthony, you need to g—"

Bang! "No, you listen to me! Open this door right now, you little bitch. I won't tell you again! Don't make me break down this door," he ordered. "Open up!"

"Anthony," Nazariah called out to him calmly. "You need to leave before I call the cops."

"Oh, so you're going to call the cops on me?" he questioned her curiously. "The love of your life? The man that's done everything and anything to make you happy."

"Anthony, you're not the love of my life! You really need to go!"

"I ain't going anywhere, bitch! Open this motherfucking door, right fucking now. Right now, bitch!"

"Anthony, just go! Leave me alone!"

"Shut the hell up and open the door bi... What the fuck... Whoa, chill man! I'm here to see my girl."

Nazariah's ears were now glued to what was happening on the other side of her door. By the sounds of things, someone had joined Anthony.

"You mean *my* girl?"

Hearing his deep baritone all of a sudden sent a shiver down her spine and an electrifying feeling down to her below.

"What the... Hassan? What are you doing here, man? Put the gun away kid."

Gun?

Nazariah flung her door open after hearing that there was now a gun involved. And upon opening it, she was greeted to Hassan's handsome face that had an irritated facial expression as he held a gun to the side of Anthony's head.

"Kid?" Hassan furiously barked before pistol whipping the side of Anthony's face. "Nigga, don't you ever fuckin' disrespect me like that ever again!"

Blood was now all over the left side of Anthony's face and Nazariah watched on with fear for Anthony. She had seen this side of Hassan before and it wasn't pretty.

"Anthony, please, just le—"

"So you've been fucking around with my cousin-in-law?!" Anthony yelled, cutting her off before she could finish speaking. "This is what you've been doing?! You little slu—"

Before Anthony could finish, Hassan had already lost it.

He simply placed his gun in the waistband of his jeans before grabbing hold of Anthony and beginning to beat him up.

Nazariah felt like she was in a dream.

The worst dream ever.

It was all happening in slow motion.

Hassan throwing punch upon punch onto Anthony's bloody face. Hassan pinning him to the floor. Kicking his chest, legs and wherever else he could.

Nazariah's worst nightmare.

"Hassan, stop! Stop, Hassan! You're going to kill him!" she cried, trying to pull him away.

But it was no use.

Hassan's anger couldn't be contained. He had already heard Anthony call his woman out of her name. First with bitch and just before he could finish off calling her a slut, Hassan knew he had to be the one to teach him a lesson.

He wasn't about to show him any mercy for disrespecting what belonged to him. No one disrespected what belonged to him.

"Hassan, please! STOP!"

Hassan wasn't listening to her though.

MISS JENESEQUA

$ CHAPTER TWENTY-TWO $

Amina felt Khyree push himself closer to her so that his hard chest was pressed against her back. Their fingers were intertwined together in front of Amina, and his lips were romantically kissing on her skin.

As great as it felt, cuddling in bed with her boo after some out of this world sex, Amina was still so nervous and worried. She knew that if there was any other time to let Khyree know about her pregnancy, it was now.

"Khy... There's something I need to let you know."

"Hmm," he moaned quietly, planting one last kiss on her skin before coming up and looking down at her. Those attractive brown eyes of his now filled with so much wonder. "What is it, beautiful?"

"I'm pregnant," she quickly blurted out. She didn't want to drag things out and create a big dramatic scene over it. She just wanted to get things over and done with.

Khyree's eyes widened with shock. "What did you say?"

"Well... I think I'm pregnant, I'm not 100% sure yet. I only took one test and it was positive. I've booked a doctor's appointment for Friday."

"Okay," he awkwardly stated. "And you're keeping it, if you are pregnant?"

Ouch.

Amina felt like a huge punch had just been thrown on her heart. He had really just asked her if she was keeping the baby. Their baby.

"What's that supposed to mean? I'm not allowed to keep it? Is that what you're trying to say?"

Khyree was truly gob smacked. He didn't know how to really feel right now. He had never gotten anyone pregnant before. He was always careful but with Amina, he just wanted things to be really intimate between them. Without the condoms.

"...I gotta be honest with you, Mina, I don't really know what to say other than I'm not really sure I'm ready to be a father. We're not ready to be parents, baby. We haven't even been together for six months yet, beautiful. Now we bringing babies into the mix?"

Amina immediately shifted away from him. "I don't believe this shit. So what you're telling me is... You want me to have an abortion?"

"Amina, I didn't sa—"

"You want me to have an abortion. Is that what you want,

320

Khyree?"

"All I want is for you, for us... to be happy," he said, pointing from her to him. "I feel like bringing a baby into the mix right now will ruin shit between us. We haven't even got deep into the relationship yet and now you might be pregnant?"

"I might be pregnant because of you!" she furiously barked. "You were the one who said, 'No condoms, beautiful. I wanna feel every last part of that tight pussy on my dick.' You remember saying that shit to me, nigga?"

"I do, and now I see that was a mistake and I—"

"Get out," she barked.

"What?" he asked her in confusion.

"Get the fuck out! I don't want you here, get out and leave me alone!"

"I'm not go—"

"Get out my house, Khyree," she cried, feeling tears fall down her cheeks. "NOW!"

She wanted him gone. He didn't want a child with her? Then she no longer wanted him.

***

Anthony was gone.

Bruised up, scared up and injured, but still gone.

Nazariah's shouting had managed to bring Hassan back to his senses. He had finally stopped beating up Anthony but the damage had already been done.

"You could have killed him," Nazariah commented in a tone laced with disappointment. "You could have killed him!"

"Well I didn't!" he fumed. "So stop yellin' at a nigga like I won't fuck you up."

"There was absolutely no need for you to do what you did tonight. Putting a gun on him! Injuring him! Now he's gonna run straight to Dominique and tell her every—"

He cut her off. "Well he can do whatever the hell he likes because Dominique ain't my responsibility anymore."

Nazariah stared at him like he had lost his damn mind, as he stood in her bedroom doorway.

"She is your responsibility," she stated. "She's your wife."

"Not anymore," he replied coolly. "I told her I'm leavin' her. My attorney's setting up the divorce papers. I'm leaving her, Nazariah."

322

Nazariah's heart skipped a beat watching as he left her doorway and began to walk towards where she was sitting on the edge of her bed.

"I'm leavin' her for you, Miss Shyness," he announced lovingly, coming to stand in front of her.

"You are?" she whispered.

"I am," he assured her with a sexy smile, before pushing her down on her bed and slowly climbing on top of her. "I love you, Nazariah Jordan, and I just want to be with you."

Before she could respond, he had locked his lips onto hers and began to tongue her down.

She was the person he wanted to be married to. No one else.

~ *The Next Morning* ~

Nazariah slowly turned around on her bed, expecting to be greeted by those gorgeous green eyes but instead of eyes, she was greeted to a note.

Miss Shyness,

I'm sorry about the shit that went down yesterday. I never wanted you to ever have to see that side of me again, but that nigga disrespected me when he disrespected you. But again, I

323

apologize. I also apologize that I can't be here with you this morning, but I promise I'll be with you later tonight. I just have some business I need to take care of, you know how it is. A nigga gotta keep working so I can buy you more diamond necklaces, right? Have a great day at work though, baby. I love you.

San x

All Nazariah could do was smile and begin to get ready for work. Even though Hassan had made love to her all last night and left her a sweet morning note, things were not resolved between them. She still wanted to discuss what he had done to Anthony and for him to properly explain how he was planning on leaving Dominique.

But all of that would have to wait because Nazariah had work to tend to.

***

"And I kicked him out. If I'm pregnant, there's no way I'm having an abortion. I don't care how long we've been together, Naz, he put his seed up in me and now can't step up? Then I don't want his ass," Amina voiced with a frown.

"Are you sure he said he wanted you to get an abortion?" Nazariah questioned suspiciously.

"Well that's what he implied, Zariah. He doesn't want the baby."

"But he loves you though. If he loves you, why would he not want the baby?"

"I honestly don't know and I really don't care. I'm over him," Amina snapped.

"You're definitely not over him, girl, you know you love him. I don't get why you haven't told him that yet. Maybe he's not nervous about the baby coming, maybe he's nervous because you haven't told him you love him. He might be thinking how he's he supposed to start a family with a woman that doesn't love him."

"I do love him," Amina admitted.

"Then you need to go ahead and tell him that," Nazariah advised gently, before taking a sip of her coffee. "Tell him you love him."

The girls were currently having their mid-day break outside by the hospital's canteen outdoor seating area. Nazariah saw this as the perfect time for Amina to stop acting stubborn, call up her man and just tell him how she really felt.

"Khy... Yeah, I just called to apologize... For kicking you out last night... Yeah, I'm sorry... I also wanted to tell you that... I love you."

Nazariah couldn't help but smile with happiness seeing the way Amina's face had lit up with joy.

"You want the baby, Khy? Are you sure?... What if I'm not pregnant, Khy? You said yourself, we're not ready... Okay... Okay, but I really do love you... I know, I was just scared to say it back... Okay baby, alright, I hear you... I'll see you later then, handsome... I love you too, bye."

Amina hung up the call before sighing deeply and looking at Nazariah with happy eyes.

"He said he loves me and wants to be with me regardless if there's a baby or not. He thought I didn't love him."

"See, girl, what did I say?" Nazariah asked her knowingly. "You guys are going to be just fine. You're fine! You guys just need to have a really deep conversation and that's it."

Amina nodded confidently before grabbing her coffee on the table in front of her.

"But you and Hassan? You said he beat up Anthony?"

"Yeah, he did," Nazariah replied in an upset tone, avoiding eye contact with Amina as she said it, so that she was observing the outdoor hospital greenery and outdoor parking space. "It's like

326

he's a whole other..."

Her words quietly trailed off once she spotted a black sedan pull up into the parking lot.

Curiosity made her continue to look on at it as it drove in ferociously and stopped a few distances away from where Amina and Nazariah currently sat on their separate table.

Nazariah observed the car carefully, thinking that maybe someone had come to drop off a patient or worker of the hospital.

But she thought absolutely wrong.

The tinted car windows slowly rolled down and that's when Nazariah spotted it.

The barrel of a silver gun. A 10mm to be exact.

Her heart instantly stopped and everything suddenly happened so fast. All she remembered doing was yelling at Amina to duck and take cover, before doing it herself.

Then the shots were fired.

Bang! Bang! Bang!

One by one.

Bang! Bang! Bang!

All flying in their direction.

Bang! Bang! Bang!

Then the sound of tires screeching and the sedan driving off was heard.

Nazariah's ears were ringing from all the shots and it felt like her ears were bleeding and on fire.

The shock of what had just played out hadn't settled into her brain yet. Until she opened her eyes and saw blood flowing near her feet.

Her eyes followed the trail of blood thinking it was from her and that she had been shot, but she didn't feel any bullets hit her. It wasn't from her.

Her breathing rapidly increased as she looked ahead only to see her best friend flat out, face down on the concrete floor, with blood leaking out of her body.

Multiple gun shots had hit Amina's body. Nazariah was speechless. Her heart only raced uncontrollably and tears began to fall out of her eyes. Amina had been shot multiple times and by the looks of things, she was no longer conscious. Only blood continued to leave her body.

"AMINA! AMINA, NO! SOMEBODY, HELP ME!

328

PLEASE!" she screamed, holding to Amina's badly shot body. She was losing a lot of blood. Her nurse scrubs were now completely stained with her blood.

Someone had just attempted to kill them both.

"PLEASE, SOMEONE HELP ME!"

But only managed to hit one target which meant that they weren't done. Whoever just shot Amina mercilessly was going to come back.

For Nazariah.

~ To Be Continued ~

~ *A Note From Miss Jen* ~

Thank you so much for reading Miss Jenesequa's novel.

Please *do not forget to drop a review on Amazon, it will be greatly appreciated and I would love to hear what you thought about this novel! Don't forget to check out her other works:*

Lustful Desires: Secrets, Sex & Lies

Sex Ain't Better Than Love 1 & 2

Luvin' Your Man: Tales Of A Side Chick

Down For My Baller 1 & 2

Bad For My Thug 1 & 2 & 3

Addicted To My Thug 1 & 2 & 3

Love Me Some You

The Thug & The Kingpin's Daughter 1 & 2

Feel free to connect with Miss Jenesequa at:

Facebook Page: Miss Jenesequa –

-   https://www.facebook.com/AuthorMis sJenesequa

And join her **readers group** *for exclusive sneak peaks of upcoming books and giveaways! A sneak peak of part two will be posted exclusively in the group so make sure you're part of it!*

https://www.facebook.com/groups/missjensreaders/

Website: www.missjenesequa.com

Please make sure to leave a review! I love reading them. Thank you so much for the support and love. I really do appreciate it.

Miss Jenesequa

Looking for a publishing home?

Royalty Publishing House, Where the Royals reside, is accepting submissions for writers in the urban fiction genre. If you're interested, submit the first 3-4 chapters with your synopsis to submissions@royaltypublishinghouse.com. Check out our website for more information: www.royaltypublishinghouse.com.

Be sure to LIKE our Royalty Publishing House

page on Facebook

MISS JENESEQUA

COMING NEXT!

Royalty Publishing House

No
MERCY
Me & My Hitta

SHAMEKA JONES

Did you grab our last #Royal release?

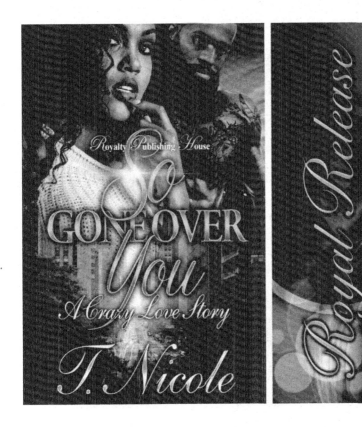

Do You Like CELEBRITY GOSSIP? Check Out

QUEEN DYNASTY!

Like Our Page <u>HERE</u>! Visit Our Site:

<u>www.thequeendynasty.com</u>

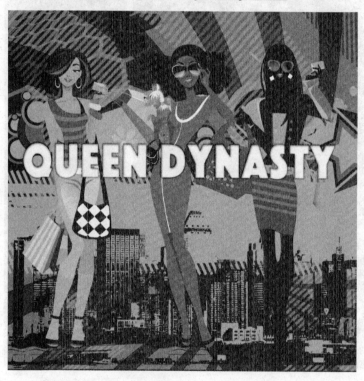

HAVE YOU CLICKED ON THESE RELEASES?

CPSIA information can be obtained
at www.ICGtesting.com
Printed in the USA
LVOW13s2305100818
586676LV00010B/104/P